EARLIE

HOLLY THORNE

For you who was there when I began
writing this book, but not by the end of it.

Earlie watched the human girl fill up her glass and wondered what it'd be like to seize the girl's arm and run her tongue from wrist to elbow. A tattoo of a rose was there, ink faded. She was still dressed in her earthly garb—ripped trousers, a belly bar turning the skin of her stomach green, eyes smudged with mascara. She had been crying, this human.

The girl moved away. Earlie picked up her glass and took a sip, eyes straying back to the vaulted hall beyond.

It was aeons now since her coming of age ceremony had been commemorated with a speech, since she'd danced over the quartzite floor with her father, smiling up into his steely eyes whilst her hair fanned around them like spun sugar, since the feast had been laid and eaten, then laid again when a troll fell into the ornately carved table, upending it over the hall floor.

That had easily been Earlie's favourite part of the revel. She'd pouted heavily when the troll was escorted from the hall, steps lumbering and drunk, arms taking clumsy thumps at the guards who held him. Cerulean had smirked; it had been her to spike the punch. Most folk had noticed the crystal bowl turning from green to red but trolls were especially dull-witted.

Blinking drowsily, Earlie caught the flicker of some being's eyes beyond the light of a candelabra. Dustings of dirt fell into her hair from above where the winged creatures glided from bough to bough. As she swiped away the grit, a low growl rumbled through the hall and Earlie caught the end of a smothered shriek.

She rested her chin in her palms; the rabble were growing restless too.

For three hours now, Earlie, her older sisters and two, stoic parents had been confined to the head table, watching the endless procession of entertainment before them. They clapped absently as a blue whisp of a girl bowed after finishing her dance. She was so tiny that Earlie found it difficult to follow the speck of her over the floor.

When a wizened fairy stepped up afterwards, carrying a fiddle, Earlie sighed, lowering her head until it landed on her sister's shoulder.

'I am so bored I might die,' she whispered. 'I am so bored that dying seems fun.'

'Dance then, Earlie,' Cerulean told her. She swept a hand over the hall where boggarts and nymphs and winged fae and horned fae all stood in the shadows, arcing around the area cleared for performers. 'Clear the hall. Send everyone away. Demand your iron necklace now. This is your night, little one.'

Earlie tipped her head back and smiled, taking in a breath of the mulchy hall air as if she could smell all the metal and concrete and flesh of the world above her.

Risarial was the only one of the sisters who had actually ventured earthside; Cerulean having only sat on Earth's curb, dangling over her legs.

Her oldest sister always returned stinking and with a headache that lasted for nights but Earlie was fascinated every time by the fire in her eyes—a fire she wanted to burn herself on, too.

Now that she was of age, Earlie was permitted to venture earthside herself. Once presented with her iron necklace, the hill above her head would crack like an egg, opening to a world of sunlight and danger and maybe—*maybe*—something more.

Earlie stood up before another performer could take the place of the fiddler. Holding a long-fingered hand up to the hall, she made her way down the table, ignoring the frown of disapproval from her mother.

Her mother who had barely left her chair all revel, only rousing to brush aside revellers caught in the snare of her beauty. Earlie passed a young pixie boy being held back by his wings, blood snaking down the veins as they teared. His obsidian eyes showed neither pain nor fear, just a manic compulsion to be close to his lady. Earlie waved a hand over his eyes to extricate him and only then did he scream.

She pushed aside the curtain of ivy and stepped out into the night. A light mizzle was falling and the youngest of the fae were gathered close against it, refusing to honour their families by engaging in the revel's formalities. Under the apple trees, a group of male fae antagonised a human servant, one holding his tray above their head and tipping the glasses atop it so they spilled. Another held a changeling girl by the hand, leading her away from her fae parent and into the trees.

Gathered too were members of the seelie court's gentry, here only because tradition demanded it. They grimaced as the hems of dresses and jackets caught on the thick brambles which arced over the garden. Earlie walked through them, her own dress gliding smoothly and snagging on nothing.

She slipped under a drape of willow, emerging onto a shadowy balcony. Leaning against the stone balustrade, Earlie peered out at the grey-blue waters. Somewhere out there, beyond all the mist and the rain and the invisible, impenetrable boundary was the human world.

'You just missed a great fight break out between the courts. All that blood was beautiful.'

Earlie turned her head as Risarial emerged on her left, lifting two hands to rest on the balustrade beside her. A long tendril of hair breezed over her forehead, quickly dotting with rain. She shook her head to dislodge it, gaze fixed on the far white band of mist.

Risarial had inherited their mother's inky hair and dark, ovoid eyes which always roved so slowly, so deliberately. Though they held none of the deathliness as their mothers', they were just as enrapturing in their intensity.

Earlie spotted a smile beginning on those red lips. She frowned and looked away. 'Rubbish.'

'Rubbish, indeed,' Cerulean said. She carried a stein of punch instead of the delicate, tall glass presented to her at the beginning of the revel. 'You miss nothing but Mother's ugly frown and a mob of cantankerous seelie courtiers.'

Earlie smiled. 'Oh dear. I am ever so rude.' Absently, she reached a hand up to her neck, trailing her fingers over where her necklace would sit.

Risarial turned so her back leant against the balustrade and eyed the path of Earlie's fingers. She said, 'You'll be a lamb thrown to wolves.'

'You go often,' Earlie countered. She moved her fingers to her hair and flicked it behind her shoulders.

'It's like slowly filling your veins up with poison.'

'Then it must be an addictive poison. Staying here will kill me faster. Boredom must be its own kind of venom.'

Risarial chuckled. Earlie caught the tang of her perfume—tuberose and amber—as she leant close and whispered into her ear, 'Then I think you are ready.'

Beside them, Cerulean frowned. 'What will you do?' She took a mouthful of punch, running the back of her hand over her lips. The golden curls in her short hair bounced as she did.

Earlie gazed down at the gently moving waters. She caught sight of the mermaids swimming just below the surface, smiling up at her and offering their watery congratulations. She let her eyes trail along their rippling hair and to the skin which was bare above their opalescent tails.

'I want to find love,' she said, looking up at her sisters. Her eyes, for the first time, held the same intensity as

Risarials'. 'Real, true, mortal love.'

Cerulean raised an eyebrow. 'Indeed?' She looked over at Risarial who had fallen still, fingers taut around the bloodstone pendent she wore at her neck. 'Is this something you've found on your travels?'

Risarial slowly shook her head. She tapped a finger down on the balustrade, lips pursed. 'The quest is oddly burdensome.'

'How so?' Earlie asked.

Risarial smiled thinly. 'You will soon find out for yourself. Humans…they're complicated little creatures. Messy. Exasperating.'

Cerulean laughed aloud. 'You mean to say they're all impervious to your charm.'

Risarial glared, brown eyes burning orange for a fleeting second. She breathed out slowly through her nose. 'Okay then,' she said quietly. She took Cerulean's stein and lifted it high. 'A bargain. For all of us to find love—mortal love. Now we're all of the same pecking order, it's only fair we garner up a little competition between ourselves.'

Cerulean stood up straight and folded her muscular arms. 'Go on,' she said, blue eyes sparkling with interest.

'We each go earthside, alone. One by one. Earlie first.' She cut her eyes to Earlie who stood with steepled fingers pressed against her lips as if she couldn't quite contain herself. 'See if we can't temper some of that excitement of yours.'

'What are the rules?' Earlie whispered.

Risarial closed her eyes for a moment. When she opened them again, she looked between her sisters and said to them the words,

> *One by one, we go alone,*
> *above the dirt and worms and bone,*
> *to find a maiden fair and true,*
> *to fill her heart with love and rue.*
> *And when we return to under the hill,*
> *her memories gone but our ghost there still…*

CHAPTER 1

Kenzie sat with her feet submerged in a stream, watching the silt play over her ankles. In her hands were twigs which she broke into smaller pieces before flicking into the water. She counted five seconds before they were whisked around a bend and out of sight.

On the other side of the bank, her lab Jenkins troughed through the wet mud like a truffle pig.

It was dark and damp here under the trees but beyond their branches, Kenzie could see a field bleached lime green by sunlight. Planting her palms, she leant her head back, letting the dappled light play over her skin.

After a time, Jenkins came to nose at her scalp. 'You done, mate?' She retracted her feet from the water and stood up. 'Come on then. Let's go get drinkies.'

It was a half hour walk back down the canal path and up the cobbled hill to their end-terrace cottage. It was hot—too hot really, for Jenkins to be out—but the walk along the water was mostly under shade. She passed a few walkers, tourists most likely, and more than a few gaggles of geese, before emerging onto the backstreet which housed the library and the town's oldest pub. A man in a bucket hat sat at an outside table, a sweating pint in front of him. He nodded at Jenkins as he passed and Kenzie saw that most of his teeth were either black or entirely missing.

The high street was thronged with people walking along the narrow, bunting-strewn pavements. Kenzie stabbed at the button for the pedestrian crossing. The flow of traffic was moving slow enough, the roads clogged with day visitors and those passing through to the larger cities, but Kenzie didn't want to chance it with Jenkins. The dog was well-enough behaved off lead but, as her mum's fond of saying, it only takes that one time.

'Come on then,' Kenzie said, clapping her hands to let Jenkins know it was okay to cross. The lab bounded across the road and started up the steep hill to the cottage.

The front door was unlocked when she reached it. Fanning her face with a palm, she plonked herself down on the bottom step in the hallway to remove her trainers. Kicking them to the side, she walked through to the kitchen where her mum, wearing her biggest, airiest dress, poured lemonade from a pitcher she'd made up that morning.

'Got nice colour in your cheeks, there,' she said, smiling at Kenzie's flushed face. Her own short, thick hair was damp at the edges. 'Sun's really brought out your freckles. Want an ice-lolly or something, love?'

'Oh, yeah. That'd be nice. Bloody boiling out there.'

Kenzie sat down heavily at the small dining table, listening to Jenkins gulp loudly from his water bowl. She pinched her t-shirt and flapped it away from her skin, feeling the sweat pooling in the curves of her waist. Fortunately, she was wearing swimming trunks on the bottom which helped wick up some of the dampness.

'Orange or cola?' Her mum stooped, sticking her head in the freezer. 'Oh,' she moaned, 'that's nice. Could just crawl in there.'

'Not got any strawberry?'

'No, you ate all of them greedy guts.'

'Cola then, please.'

Kenzie took her ice-lolly and went to stand in the back doorway, where a small breeze was blowing. The small garden beyond waved merrily, wildflowers and weeds and herbs blooming in abundance.

Kenzie's mum wasn't much into cultivated lawns. She

liked the bees and the butterflies and the little sparrows which splashed in her bird bath. It was made up in weathered stone; a fairy girl holding a large shell above her head. There were fairy adornments tacked to the back fence too, catching the sun through their stained-glass bodies and throwing a kaleidoscope of colours over the wood.

It wasn't unusual decor for Kirkall Bridge, a town steeped in folklore ever since Harmon Blythe published a volume on fairy sightings and encounters in the area way back when.

This day and age, it was all considered tosh—mostly—but it made for good tourism; there were fairy trails for the kids and museum exhibitions and folklore plays put on at the park during the summer months.

Something the town milked for all it was worth, anyway. If it wasn't for that shiny piece of history, Kenzie reckoned it would just be a waster town like all the other towns dotted up and down this stretch of canal.

Kenzie sucked the last of the liquid from her lolly wrapper and tossed it into the bin, batting away the fruit flies who had congregated there. 'I'm gonna have a shower.'

'Alright, love.' Her mum looked up from where she was rinsing a bowl of plums over the sink. 'Wouldn't stay up there too long, mind. It's a bloomin' oven.'

Grimacing, Kenzie left the kitchen. Jenkins raised his head like he wanted to follow but seemed to think better of it and flopped back down on the kitchen tile again.

After a cold shower, Kenzie entered her bedroom. The curtains had been drawn to protect against the midday sun but the room was still stifling.

From her drawers, she plucked a pair of shorts and a plain t-shirt which belonged to her dad before she'd nabbed it. It was a little baggy on her—her dad was a big guy—but she didn't mind.

Wandering over to her desk, Kenzie toggled the mouse of her laptop until the screen turned on. Sprawled next to it were all her documents for university. She was due to start at Manchester Met in September and was still finalising a few things. The uni still hadn't let her know where she'd be staying for the year and it was beginning to nag at her.

Seeing no new emails, Kenzie blew out a raspberry and closed the laptop. The curtains behind the desk were blowing lightly towards her, making the edges of the documents flutter. She reached out and pulled them aside. The street below, a good distance from the main road, was empty apart from a gaggle of topless boys who ambled past wheeling bikes towards the woods at the end of the road.

She was due to work the fairy trail there, day after next. It was something she'd done last summer for a bit of extra cash and it turned out to be a pretty fun job. She still had some bits and bobs to buy for her new place, wherever that was going to be, so the money definitely wouldn't go amiss.

It was supposed to cool off a bit, too, and they'd been promised thunder towards the end of the week. Looking at the crystal-clear skies now, it was difficult to imagine them choking up with storm clouds.

CHAPTER 2

The night was muggy and hot and dank. Earlie stood on the crest of the hill, overlooking the black countryside. Her keen senses could feel the worms coiling in the grasses, the owls scanning the ground and the thready heartbeats of the mice they pursued. Her mouth was open, gulping in the heavy air and her eyes were fixed on all the tiny lights flickering in the valley below.

Her neck was bare of the iron necklace now, two nights and two days after the revel, but she could still feel the throb of it there. Though it had been heavily coated, the weighty, shackle-like chain had still burnt into her skin, leaving a welt as thick as two fingers.

Cerulean had had to hold her still as she'd screamed and bayed, begging for it to be taken off. If they had, she'd have been slaughtered then and there. The court forbade weakness.

Now, she bore the mark proudly. A token to show that though fae-kind dwelled below the earth, they still, and would forever, reign supreme.

Remembering this, Earlie took her first step down the hill.

CHAPTER 3

The train station was baking. Kenzie leant back against a support, eyeing the mouth of the tunnel where her train was to emerge. It was five minutes late already and Kenzie was only glad the station sat mostly in shade.

She'd deliberated over driving to Leeds, instead of taking the train, but the need for a cold one in a pub garden was almost overwhelming.

Finally, the nose of the train appeared and Kenzie shuffled forwards with the rest of the passengers waiting to board.

After making sure all the windows in her carriage were open, Kenzie sat herself at a table seat. She removed her snapback and laid it next to her phone, rifling her hands through her sweaty brown hair. It needed a cut; it was almost touching her shoulders now.

After shooting off a message to the friend she was meeting, she sat back in her seat as the train pulled out of the station.

It was a journey she'd taken countless times, the whole way through secondary school and college after that. Kirkall Bridge only had a primary school so Kenzie and the rest of the kids her age had had to travel to school once they'd turned eleven. It meant most of her friends lived an hour away, which felt like a faff until she'd learnt to drive.

It wasn't an awful journey, one she appreciated more the older she got. Once they got past the long stretch of tall green banks choked with brambles and dumped rubbish, the train emerged into the rolling hills of the countryside surrounding Kirkall. It was the hill to the east, the only one which bloomed with purple heather come August, that Blythe had set the scene for his fairy lore.

The first day of secondary school, the only time Kenzie's mum had come on the train with her, she'd been told the story. She remembered spending most of the year with her face glued to the window whenever they came to the hill.

As the years passed though, her fascination naturally waned. Trading snacks with the older kids and keeping an eye out for the pretty conductor she had a crush on suddenly seemed much more important.

Today though, with the sun shining down on the first flushes of purple dotting the knoll, Kenzie found her eyes drawn to it again, wrapped up in the magical nostalgia she used to feel as a kid.

❧ ❧

Holding her pint away from her, Kenzie made her way out into the beer garden. It was busy, packed with students and locals belonging to Leeds' queer community. She finally spotted Asa at the back, sitting beneath a parasol.

'Aye, aye,' she said, plopping her cider down on the table.

Asa grinned up at her with his usual thin-lipped, bashful smile. Since Kenzie had last seen him, he'd bleached his dark hair and sported a new septum piercing.

'I already got you one, pal,' he replied, pushing a second pint towards her.

'Ah well. More for me.' She saluted him with her glass. 'I like the do.'

'Thanks.' Asa reached up and touched his hair gingerly, eyes roving the beer garden. He turned back to Kenzie, leant in close and said, 'Pissin' Aaron's here, isn't he.'

Under the guise of taking a sip from her glass, Kenzie

looked around the beer garden 'Where?'

'He was here a minute ago, at the foosball table over there.'

Though she tried, Kenzie couldn't spot the carefully combed head belonging to Asa's ex. She was kind of glad—she'd always hated that hairdo, even more so since he'd broken up with her best friend and left her to pick up the pieces. 'Who was he with?'

Asa shrugged. 'Some girl. Imagine if he was with another guy though.'

'Well he wasn't so don't think about it.'

'Yeah. But hey, the girl was cute though.' Asa waggled his eyebrows. He'd bleached them too; it was a marvel they hadn't singed off. 'Your type.'

Kenzie smiled. 'Oh, yeah?'

'Yeah, pretty and straight-looking.'

Kenzie laughed. 'Probably definitely straight then.'

'Probs.' Asa picked up his pint and swirled it. Condensation from the glass dripped onto the table. 'So how's uni prep going? Excited yet? I'm still pissed you're not going to Leeds, you know.'

'Sorry, would have if I could, but they don't do my course, do they?'

'Well, you better invite me for some big gay nights out.'

'Hell yeah.' She smiled. 'Don't worry. And yeah, it's going alright. Mum's all sad and stuff but...' Kenzie shrugged.

Asa pouted his lips. 'Her baby all going away. I know how she feels.'

Kenzie rolled her eyes. 'She'll be fine. I'll hardly be on the other side of the world, will I?'

'I always pull more in Manchester than here anyway,' Asa said. His cheeks dimpled as he grinned.

'Let's hope it's the same with me. Kirkall's just fucking...' Kenzie shook her head.

'Dry? Well, just you remember'—Asa raised his pint to her—'no shagging your flatmates. Messy business, that.'

Nodding solemnly, Kenzie put a hand to her chest. 'I will try my best not to.'

CHAPTER 4

Earlie stared hard at the reflective glass window, oblivious to all the people sidestepping around her on the pavement.

All the way down to this dry, stinky, hot place, she had gathered her glamour around her. Her fingers were still tingling, dripping with the residual magic that continued to flow through her. She fluttered them and took a step closer to her reflection.

She was inches shorter now, her face less oval. She'd donned her plainest, most drab dress, made from the silkworms the sylphs cultivated. It clung to her slender frame and rippled in the breeze around her thighs.

'A picture would last longer, love.'

In the glass, Earlie saw two human boys loitering outside the shop she was peering into. They each held a bottle in their hands and their chests were bare, t-shirts hanging limp over their shoulders.

'Yeah, I'll take one for you,' the second said, hiding his smirk behind his bottle.

Earlie turned carefully. As they took a step closer, her nose twitched at the stench of them. Their hearts pounded thickly like bubbles in a cauldron, their blood sluggish as it moved through their veins.

'Mate, look at her,' the taller one said, squinting in the sunlight. 'She's high as fuck. Look at her eyes.'

Reaching up, Earlie touched beneath her eyes with the

pads of her fingers. She wasn't sure what was wrong with them. The glamour had filmed over their lilac colour and Risarial had assured her that the fine glitter which clung to her eyelashes and brows would look like human makeup.

Eventually, the boys left. Earlie could feel their disconcertion and felt a rush of irritation. She wanted to fit in, she was trying. For a time, she wanted to be one of *them*.

Turning in a pirouette, Earlie regarded the path she stood on. Right would take her the way the boys had gone, to where people were sitting at tables and eating food or walking around holding bags. On her left was the sanctuary of the forest.

Taking in a breath through her nose, Earlie retreated to the left.

CHAPTER 5

Kenzie chased Jenkins around the kitchen, brandishing a pair of fairy wings she was bent on putting on him. She'd done the same thing last year on a whim and the kids had loved it. Now though, the dog was having none of it. Seeing her lunge for him again, he barked, ducked his head then bounded away.

'Jenkins! God's sake, I'm not going to hurt you. Come here! Dude, I'm not trying to play a game.'

Finally, she wrangled him in the corner of the kitchen and got the straps under his legs. The silver-rimmed wings flopped over his back and she righted them. After ensuring the dog wasn't about to try and pull the things off, she straightened up and picked up his lead. The organisers of the trail encouraged volunteers to don fairy attire but Kenzie wasn't exactly the delicate, pink-wearing type.

'You good lad,' she told Jenkins, giving him a scratch behind the ears. 'You ready?'

Kenzie left the kitchen and walked to the bottom of the stairs. 'Mum?' she called, sitting down to pull on her trainers. 'I'm off.'

'Okay, love. You taking the dog?'

'Yeah, be back in an hour or so.'

Kenzie let Jenkins out the front door and locked up, slipping the key into the back pocket of her shorts and starting off up the road towards the woods. It was cooler today, though only just, and Kenzie was happy the tour took place in the woods where it was shady and damp.

She let Jenkins wander around first, getting all his sniffs and wees out before taking the path which led down to the small nature reserve housing the fairy trail during the summer months. It wasn't the exact location as detailed by Blythe but was still in the same stretch of woods.

Kenzie pulled on her volunteer hi-vis vest and unfurled the trail worksheets she had tucked under her arm. She could see a couple of families milling around the sign which read, *WAIT HERE FOR THE FAIRY TRAIL.*

After introducing herself and Jenkins—'He's actually a fairy in disguise, you know'—and taking donations, she handed out the sheets to the kids.

'Keep an eye out for the fairies,' she instructed, handing them all a pencil each. 'And when you see one, tick them off here. Just remember not to be too loud or you'll scare them off. They're easily spooked, these ones.'

Some of the parents looked at her appreciatively for that. As the kids skipped off to look for fairies, Kenzie began regaling the truer, darker history of the woods, beginning with the tale of the October Imp. It was one of her favourites—she could get down with all the little sprites who lived to cause mischief to humans.

Once she'd finished, a burly man asked, 'Lived here all your life then, duck?' In his arms was a toddler who gripped the worksheet in a closed chubby fist.

Kenzie nodded. 'Born and raised.'

'And have you ever seen a fairy?' The man smiled.

'No,' Kenzie said, chuckling. 'Afraid not. Maybe today will be the day.'

As the kids ran around the reserve, Kenzie answered questions on the local area. They moved into the more sheltered part of the woods, where the trees leaned into each other to create a shadowy avenue.

'I always did wonder about fairies, or the fae, whatever you call them,' one of the women was saying. 'My granny, when she was alive—batty old thing she was—she was from

24

Ireland and always referred to them as the fair folk, or the wee folk. They weren't like this though.' The woman gestured to Jenkins' wings which batted up and down as he trotted alongside them. 'They were *mean*. They would lure new mams away and steal babies and take men to be their servants.' The woman gave a shiver. 'I much prefer the sweet, cherubic types myself.'

Kenzie nodded. 'Kind of like Harmon Blythes' fairies. In his book there's tales like that. Fairies that would drug humans and what-not. It's a really interesting read. Not that long, either.'

'Are you pitching to us?' one of the dads joked, a behatted man with thick-rimmed glasses.

Kenzie shrugged and offered him a smile. 'There's a load in the visitor centre if you're interested.'

They turned a corner on the trail. Up ahead, the kids were clustered around one spot, looking down at their worksheets and back into the trees. Kenzie knew from memory there wasn't a fairy tacked to any tree there. As she got closer, she spotted a very slender, very pale leg hooked over a branch. The girl, when she reached her, was sitting on a low bough, smiling at the children who were clustered around her. When they saw Kenzie and the adults, they disbanded, whispering amongst themselves and sneaking back glances.

'Ah!' the burly man boomed. 'Are you a fairy then?'

The girl's smile faded and she pursed her lips. 'How could you tell?'

'Well for starters, only a fairy would wear that kind of dress around all this mud. Coulda done with a pair of wings, love.' The man turned back to Kenzie. 'Did you plant her?'

Kenzie opened her mouth to reply but closed it again when, at her legs, Jenkins began to growl. 'Hey!' She hooked a hand around his collar and tugged. 'Sorry,' she said to the girl. 'Think you made him jump.'

The girl peered down at Jenkins dispassionately then regarded Kenzie with the same expression.

'Go on,' Kenzie said, giving the dog a push down the path. The others followed. After offering another 'sorry' to the girl, Kenzie caught up to them.

'That was great,' the burly man chortled. He looked down at Jenkins and said, 'I was almost convinced.'

Kenzie nodded. When she glanced back, the girl was facing her, lounging over the branch with her hands tucked beneath her face. This time, there was a tiny smile on her lips. Kenzie could feel heat in her cheeks and knew it would show under her fair skin. Sighing, she reached a palm up to rub at them. She felt better once they rounded another bend out of sight.

CHAPTER 6

The park between the train station and the canal was swarming with people; picnickers and kids playing in the playground and people who'd hired the big clunky bikes from the station to cycle around the nice flat pavements.

Next to the bank where Kenzie was sitting was the skate park, where groups of teens lined the edges of the ramps, every so often throwing down their skateboard or scooter to have a go themselves.

Kenzie had spent loads of time there herself over the years until a messy touchdown landed her with a nasty break to the ankle. It had taken forever to heal and put her off skateboarding at the park pretty much for good. At times, her ankle still twinged.

Kenzie watched as a younger kid hit the ground hard, her skateboard skittering off in the opposite direction. When she got back up with minimal fanfare, Kenzie turned back to the journal she had lying open over her lap.

It'd been months since she'd written in it. Every year for Christmas her mum got her a new one and with it, a renewed determination to keep the ritual up. She barely ever made it to spring. Today though, after returning from her tour, she felt strangely compelled to add an entry.

She poised her pen over the page then wrote,

I met this girl today—

Kenzie stopped. It was foolish, she was foolish. She hadn't even talked to the girl in the tree, the one with the incredibly large blue eyes and see-through dress. She hadn't been wearing a bra. Kenzie couldn't get the vision out of her head.

Her phone pinged, breaking her reverie. She could feel that heat in her face again as she opened the message—a group chat with all the teens her age in the area.

Hey Kirkall gang, it read, *we're thinking of doing a campout tomorrow before the weather gets shitty again. We need to have as many as possible before some of yous piss off to uni or wherever. As always, BYOB and more the merrier xxx*

Kenzie sent a thumbs up to show she'd be going. She hadn't any plans for that night and it had been ages since her last shindig in the woods just outside of town. It was far enough away from meddling locals and close enough to farmers who didn't care if they used their fields.

She shot Asa off a message, inviting him along, then turned back to her diary entry. It didn't seem so appealing now. She closed the journal and slipped it back into her bag.

∂> ∾

It was still light out when Kenzie picked Asa up from the last train from Leeds the following night. He caried his tent bag on his shoulder and in his hand was a bottle of vodka. A quarter of it was gone already.

'Ayup,' he greeted, slinging an arm around her shoulders.

'Started without me, I see.'

'Catch up.'

He passed her the bottle and she took a sip.

'Just need to pick up my stuff from mine then we can go,' she said.

From the hallway, Kenzie grabbed her tent bag then ousted Asa from the house before her mum could accost him with her natter. They walked up to the end of the road and into the woods.

'Man, this small-town life isn't bad this time of year, is it?' Asa craned his head, looking at the late sun shining through the canopy.

Kenzie smirked. 'Can't imagine you as a country bumpkin somehow.'

'Fuck no. But this is nice.'

It took them about twenty-five minutes to reach the clearing the campout was hosted on, by which time Asa was breathing heavily in the evening heat, sweat sheening his forehead and dragging his short fringe into pointy tendrils.

'Is that it?' He nodded towards the people milling in the field. 'Please tell me that's it. I'm dying over here.'

Kenzie rolled her eyes. 'So much for small-town life then. Let's go over there and set up the tents. Better to do it now than when we're pissed later.'

By the time they'd finished faffing around with their cheap popup tents, someone had set up speakers and was blasting house music across the field which was slowly filling up with teens.

'More like it,' Asa said, drifting towards the small cornucopia of beer cans and alcopops. After snagging one, he turned and pulled Kenzie by her hand. 'Dance with me, darl'. Since I won't be pulling tonight, you'll have to do.'

They were the only ones dancing this early in the night but Kenzie didn't care. There was no such thing as bad dancing when you did it confidently.

Though he danced with her, Asa spent more time spying on the people around them. 'So you're saying there's no one here you're even a little bit interested in?'

'No one. Plus, I'm off to uni soon so no point getting involved even if there was.'

'Yeah but someone for short term. That's still months away.'

Kenzie laughed. 'There's literally no one mate, I'm telling you.'

'Only gay in the village?'

'Close.' She teetered her head. 'Let's just say there's no one here I'd want to get involved with *again*.'

Asa looked around with renewed interest. 'Any of your

exes here then?'

Kenzie sighed and looked around too. 'That one, over there,' she said, pointing. 'With the blonde hair. Sierra. But we were literally like fourteen/fifteen. We're just friends now. She's the one who invited us out here tonight.'

'Interesting,' Asa murmured, watching the girl Kenzie had pointed to. She was laughing loudly with a boy with long hair, a bottle in her hand. 'Let me know if we see anymore.'

They did, but Kenzie wasn't about to point out the boy she'd lost her virginity to. He hadn't so much as glanced in her direction since she came out as lesbian three years ago. That was fine by her. Some things were better left forgotten.

❧ ❦

By the time the sun went down, the clearing was full of teenagers and a sizeable pile of alcohol stood in the middle of it.

'I've changed my mind,' Asa said into her ear. The music was so loud she could barely hear him. 'I love country life.'

Kenzie laughed. She had a good buzz going herself and the evening had finally cooled off to a comfortable temperature.

She'd introduced Asa to some of her friends and they all danced together around a pile of branches some of the boys had gathered together. It was intended for a fire but they hadn't been able to light it. Probably a good thing that they hadn't; the kindling was only feet from the stack of alcohol.

When Kenzie finished her latest beer, she crinkled the can and threw it to the grass. Gesturing Asa towards her, she said into his ear, 'I'm going to pee. Be right back.'

He waved her off and she stumbled towards the woodland boundary. Hopping the fence, she pulled her phone out of her pocket and turned on its torch. After arcing it around to make sure no one was near, she came to squat in a little thicket of trees.

A few seconds in, she heard the snapping of twigs.

Knowing she was pretty hidden from prying eyes, Kenzie stayed where she was, peering through the shrubbery. A dark form passed in front of her. Kenzie could see it was a girl, her body silhouetted against the small amount of light the sky still held.

As quietly as she could, she pulled up her shorts and took a step forward. The girl turned, and Kenzie saw instantly that it was the same one from the fairy trail. Her heart jumped.

'Oh, hey,' she said. The girl tilted her head, regarding her with a stillness which was almost eerie. 'I remember you from earlier.' Kenzie took a few steps closer, picking her way over nettles and thistles. 'Are you holidaying here or something? I don't think I recognise you.'

Kenzie stopped in front of her and smiled, feeling a sudden need to rectify her earlier bumbling.

'I remember you too,' the girl said, gaze fixed on Kenzie. In the indirect light of Kenzie's phone, her eyes almost glittered. 'I am a visitor here.'

'On your own or with family?'

'My own. My own, this time.'

Kenzie nodded. 'Sweet.' Buoyed by the alcohol and the darkness, she went on, 'Well you know, if you need a guide, that's kind of my job around here, so.'

At her offer, a smiled bloomed on the girl's face and she nodded keenly. 'A guide. I would love for you to be my guide.'

For a moment, Kenzie was taken aback by her eagerness, at complete odds to her impassivity on the fairy trail, and her stillness just now. She quickly returned the smile and gestured towards the field. 'Cool. Do you want to come join in? No worries if you're on your way to somewhere or whatever.'

The girl stepped up to the fence, curling her hands around the rotting top rail. 'Like a fae revel,' she said softly.

Kenzie looked at the partiers and chuckled. 'Doing their best impression, aren't they? Come on. I'll introduce you to my friends. I'm Kenzie, by the way.' When the girl failed to return her own name, Kenzie glanced at her and tried again. 'What did you say your name was?'

'You may call me Earlie,' she replied.

Kenzie nodded. Bit of a weird one, but maybe the girl had hippie parents or something. She definitely looked the type. She'd be cold later, too, still dressed in that slip of a dress.

'So, how long are you here for?' Kenzie saw Asa peering over, smirking between the two of them. She did her best to ignore him.

'When night comes quicker and leaves tinge brown; the birds fly away and the ivy now crowns.'

Kenzie blew out a breath. 'Does that mean all summer?' she hazarded a guess.

'Exactly.'

'Plenty of time,' she said, feeling a rush of something she couldn't quite place.

'Plenty, indeed.'

Before they reached Asa, Earlie took one hopping skip and then was away twirling around the cornucopia, her dress lifting dangerously high as she reached her arms towards the sky. Kenzie watched on, bemused and maybe a little embarrassed for her.

'Who the fuck is that?' Asa asked, coming to her side.

Kenzie shook her head. 'Dunno. Only just met her.'

'She's feral.'

Kenzie nudged him. 'She's having a good time. I'm drunk enough to join her, how about you?'

Asa looked around self-consciously. 'Well, since there's no fitties around here,' he said, giving a little sniff.

Kenzie grinned. When Earlie passed them again, latching onto Kenzie's hand, the two of them joined in, bounding around in a large circle.

It was kind of erratic, dancing like that to the fitful beats of the house music. After only a few minutes, Kenzie had to stop.

Claiming a bottle of something blue, she sat down a few paces away and watched. Other people were watching too, particularly the male variety. Kenzie felt like rolling her eyes. At least Asa wasn't a threat. Each time he reached out to touch Earlie, to take her hand or pull her in for one of his signature scandalous dances, she pirouetted away from him. Every so often, she'd find Kenzie's eyes through the dark and smile.

She was kind of feral, Asa was right, but Kenzie decided she liked it. Her waist-length hair was wild and knotted from her dancing, weaved with tiny plaits and shimmering threads of silver. She kept her eyes closed most of the time, the fine glitter she'd put on her eyelids dusting her cheeks like a moth's wing.

Kenzie set her bottle down on the grass and leaned back on her hands. Her heart still beat wildly and she felt a high she hadn't felt in the longest time. She was trapped in a moment she wished would go on forever.

CHAPTER 7

Kenzie peeled back the flap of the tent, letting Earlie go in before her. She heard Asa call a goodnight to them before disappearing into his own next door. He'd made a point of pulling his tent further away, letting Kenzie know exactly what he thought was about to transpire in hers.

Earlie entered hesitantly, her nose immediately crinkling. 'That smell,' she said.

Kenzie looked around. 'What, that plasticky-tent smell? Yeah, it is pretty strong.'

Kenzie reached back to rezip the door.

'No, don't,' Earlie said, putting a hand on Kenzie's forearm. 'Leave it open. I can't abide the smell.'

Kenzie pursed her lips. 'Okay.' She found the door ties and knotted the flap open. 'That okay?'

Earlie nodded. Kenzie was glad she had the foresight to angle the front of the tent towards the abandoned farmer's field rather than the clearing which was dotted with tents and the odd partier who was still awake.

When Kenzie laid back, Earlie did too. They faced the pitch-black field. In only an hour, the sun would begin to lighten the sky again.

Kenzie fought back a yawn. 'Are you tired?' she asked, turning her head.

'No,' Earlie replied. 'I feel wondrously alive.'

Kenzie smiled, her brow slightly furrowed. Earlie didn't look the least bit tired, her eyes wide open and mostly unblinking. It made her wonder if she hadn't taken a little something earlier. Plenty of that went around at campouts like these. Not her jam, but she wasn't one to judge.

She turned on her side, pillowing her head on her hands. 'How come you're here?' she asked.

'Here? Above the hill?'

'Here, in Kirkall Bridge.'

'It's where the wind landed me.'

Kenzie chuckled sleepily. 'Guess there's worse places.'

'Oh really? I would maybe like to see those places, too.'

'I'll take you, then.' Kenzie yawned again. 'Up to Ackinton. That could be fun.'

'Ackinton,' Earlie repeated.

'Mm. Up the canal. Hey, are you cold?'

Earlie came to lie on her side too, their faces scant inches apart. 'Not at all.'

Kenzie reached out and touched her fingers to Earlie's cheeks. They came away shimmery. 'Well, let me know if you do get cold. I have a hoodie packed.'

Earlie nodded. Kenzie thought she was smiling, but it was hard to tell. Her face was like the Mona Lisa's sometimes. Kenzie held herself still as one of Earlie's hands came close to her. She spread her fingers and whispered them down Kenzie's face, making her eyelids flutter shut.

'Sleep now, little human.'

Powerless to resist, Kenzie did.

જ જ

The world was muddled when she next awoke. There was light—gold, blinding light pouring in through the open tent door. Moaning lightly, Kenzie lifted her head from where it rested on her backpack. She blinked her eyes, willing them to focus. Before her, the farmer's field stretched out for eternity, the sun staining the grass gold as it breeched the horizon.

That it was sunrise was the first thing Kenzie noted.

36

Next was the memory of the strange girl she'd shared her tent with. She could see her now, just a fuzzy, gilded silhouette in the middle of the field. She didn't seem to be wearing her dress anymore.

Kenzie dropped her head back down. It felt like it weighed a million tonnes. Blinking slowly, she watched the languid dance playing out in front of her. Earlie raised her face to the sun, then her arms. When the girl turned towards her, Kenzie's eyes fell shut and she slept again, this time dreaming of dandelions and fireflies.

CHAPTER 8

'You gonna be in a mardy all morning?'

Kenzie sighed and picked up her mug of coffee. 'I'm not.'

'Bollocks aren't you.' Asa reached over and swiped a crispy potato from her plate.

Kenzie pushed the whole thing towards him, the smell of food making her feel sick to her stomach. 'I'm just hungover, alright?'

'Yeah, hungover and mad that girl from last night didn't say goodbye.'

'Well it's just annoying. She could've said something.'

'Well, she didn't. So get over it.'

Kenzie nodded. 'I will. Sorry.'

'S'okay.' Asa took a sip of his tea, his other hand reaching up to play with his nose piercing.

After cleaning up the remnants of last night's party, they'd fallen into the nearest café on the way home, ordering the stodgiest thing on the menu. A couple of other teens from the campout were there too, sopping up the alcohol with fry-ups and caffeine.

'So you're telling me nothing happened last night?' Asa pressed.

Kenzie shook her head. 'I don't even remember falling asleep.'

'*Pfft*. Wasted opportunity.'

'Well, I'm not mad. Would feel even crappier if I had.'

'Fair.' Asa picked up his phone and noted the time. 'Only got fifteen minutes until the train.'

Kenzie nodded and pushed her chair back. 'Yeah, let's go.'

After she'd dropped Asa off at the station, she took a slow mooch home, stopping off at the shops to nab herself an ice-cold smoothie, something she always craved when she was hungover. Not that she was hungover too often, but last night seemed to have knocked her for six.

Jenkins' barking when she reached the house was like knives through the head.

'Hiya, mate,' she said, grimacing as dropped her tent bag and leant down to stroke him.

'Oh dear, you look delicate,' her mum said, coming down the stairs. She was still dressed in her dressing gown and pink fluffy slippers.

'Yeah, might have gone a bit too hard,' Kenzie admitted.

Her mum tutted. 'Go on, go have a shower. Gather your wits. I'll bring you up a cuppa.'

Kenzie dragged herself up the stairs and into her bedroom. Her mum had opened her window for her, allowing a breeze to blow in and ripple the curtains. Judging by the clouds slowly filling the sky, it looked like today was when the weather would finally cool.

Kenzie sat down at her desk and rested for a moment, chin in her palm. Idly, she picked up the pen that was lying next to her journal and tapped it on the desk.

'Here you are, love.'

Kenzie sat back so her mum could place the cup of tea on the desk in front of her.

'Ta.' She pulled it towards her.

'No problem, ducky. Now who's gonna make you tea when you bugger off to uni, hm?'

Kenzie rolled her eyes. 'I'm sure I'll get by.'

Her mum chuckled and left the room, pulling the door closed behind her.

Kenzie picked up the mug and ran the rim of it over her

lips. Her eyes were on her journal. Using one hand, she flicked to her last discarded entry. She picked up her pen again and crossed it out, then went onto the next line.

The words came easier this time. She wrote about the way the sun sank so effortlessly in the sky last night and how high she felt after only a few drinks, and how unbelievably shit she felt now.

She wasn't going to mention Earlie at all but once she started, she found she couldn't stop. She wrote about the way her dress fell loose down her body like it was made of tissue paper, and how her hair reminded her of cobwebs and how alive she'd felt just to be lying next to her in the tent.

Finally she ran out of words. She stood up and set about emptying her bag from last night. She knew if she didn't do it now, she'd only fall asleep and not get round to it for days.

Pulling out yesterday's clothes, she tossed them onto the bed. Her hoodie was stuffed right at the bottom. She grasped it and shook it out, a small scrap of paper flying from it and landing on her pillow. Kenzie scooped it up, about to throw it in the bin when she caught the message written on it.

It looked like it had been forged in mud, the brown writing scrawly but strangely decorative:

Meet me on Woden's day at sun's peak. In the golden field I will be. Waiting eagerly, Earlie.

Kenzie lowered the note and frowned. What the hell? 'Woden's day…' Snatching up her phone, Kenzie opened a search engine, her heart suddenly hammering. 'Wednesday,' she whispered, scrolling through the results. 'Sun's peak. Midday.' Golden field? That had to be the farmer's field from the campout, surely. She vaguely remembered the sunrise upon first waking that morning.

Kenzie pressed the note to her chest and blew out a breath. She raised her phone to send Asa a message, hesitated, then put it down again. For reasons she couldn't explain, she wanted to keep this to herself.

CHAPTER 9

Kenzie checked her reflection one more time before putting on her snapback. She put it on straight at first, then twizzled it so it sat backwards, then turned it back to the front again. Even then, she still wasn't sure what looked best. Deciding she didn't have time to be faffing about, Kenzie stepped away from the mirror and smoothed down the sides of her shirt before heading downstairs.

'Back later, Mum,' she called and left the house.

She checked her watch as she entered the woods. She had half an hour before midday, hoping that was what Earlie had meant. Wishing she'd gotten her number, Kenzie blew out a breath, feeling more nervous than she had in a good while.

As she turned onto the path which led to the field, a horrible thought struck that almost stopped her in her tracks.

What if this wasn't a date? Earlie hadn't said it was, and Kenzie had only offered herself as a tour guide. Shit, maybe she wasn't even gay. She hated to stereotype but Earlie hardly looked the part. But then she'd been so heavy with the eye contact the night of the campout and had always wanted to dance with her, and only her.

Kenzie slowed her steps. If this wasn't a date then she didn't want to look too keen. She worried then if she was too dressed up. She had on her nice chinos and a shirt that was kind of fancy but she didn't think any of that screamed

'I fancy you'.

Suddenly, she was at the field and it was too late to worry about any of those things. Earlie was sat atop a fence rail, clothed in a dress the colour of seafoam. Kenzie smiled and forced herself to chill out.

'Hey,' she said as she approached. 'You look great.'

Carefully, Earlie unfurled herself and stood up on her feet. 'So do you. Very handsome.'

They turned and slowly wandered along the edge of the farmer's field.

'Your note was cute,' Kenzie said. Her eyes were on the grass, on Earlie's shadow which merged into hers. It seemed elongated, stretched. 'I almost threw it in the bin.'

'Why would you do that?'

'Well, just thought it was a receipt or something. Not gonna lie, I was kind of bummed you didn't say goodbye the other night.'

Earlie chuckled. 'I said goodbye, you just weren't awake.'

'Oh. Well, I'm glad we're meeting again.' Kenzie looked around. 'So, we could go this way,' she said, pointing. 'There's a nice little trail. Or we could go that way towards the stream.'

'Or, we can go this way,' Earlie said impishly, taking Kenzie's hand and pulling her in a third direction.

'Where?' Kenzie asked, struggling to keep up. 'There's only fields that way, where everyone dumps their fridges and stuff.'

Earlie stopped and twirled until she was face to face with Kenzie. She reached up with one hand and ran it over one of Kenzie's brows. 'You need to open those pretty eyes of yours more.'

Unable to muster up a reply, Kenzie fell quiet and let Earlie lead her.

They came to the fly-tipping field. Just as Kenzie remembered, it was strangled with weeds and briars with the odd corner of a washing machine sticking up like a shark's fin.

'Reminds me of home,' Earlie said, running a finger over a thorn as they passed.

'Careful,' Kenzie murmured. 'So where is home? Where are you from?'

'Over that way,' Earlie said, pointing vaguely.

'Up north?' Kenzie asked. 'You don't sound that northern. I can't place your accent at all, actually. Do you move around a lot?'

'No. This is my first time leaving home.'

'Oh, sweet.' Kenzie dodged around a tangle of old cables. 'I'm leaving home for the first time, too. In September. Only to Manchester though. Not too far, I guess.'

'Manchester.' Earlie looked skyward like she was trying to remember something. 'I think my sister has visited there on her travels.'

'Do you have just the one? Sister, I mean.'

'I have two of them. Risarial and Cerulean.'

'Interesting names.' Kenzie smiled. 'I like yours the best.'

Earlie smiled back. She still held Kenzie's hand though they were no longer jogging. 'Do you have sisters?'

Kenzie shook her head. 'I'm an only child. Super unplanned. My mum and dad had split up by the time mum found out she was pregnant with me. My dad lives just outside Manchester. I'll be closer to him than Mum when I start uni.'

Earlie looked almost sad. 'A lonely childhood, then. Not unusual where I'm from.'

They'd reached the end of the field. Kenzie looked around. 'Do you want to loop back?'

Earlie didn't reply. She continued towards the boundary of trees marking the edge of the field. Placing her hands on one of the branches, she turned back, her face hidden in shadow. In the strange half-light, it looked as though her eyes were glowing. 'Come on.'

'You'll rip your dress,' Kenzie cautioned.

Earlie's chuckle echoed through the undergrowth.

Kenzie ducked her head and followed under the branches, swatting foliage out of her face and making sure her shirt didn't snag on anything. She tumbled out the other side feeling a whole lot more rumpled.

Rightening her shirt, and hoping she wasn't sweating under her arms, she looked around. They were in another field, this one enclosed and smaller and obviously unused. It was flooded, the water over the grass turning it a soft teal colour. Reeds and bulrushes broke the surface and dragonflies flittered between their leaves.

'Wow. Lived here all my life and had no idea this was here.'

'A hidden lake,' Earlie said, trailing a toe through the water. For the first time, Kenzie noticed that she was barefoot.

'I have a picnic blanket in my bag if you wanna go sit somewhere?'

Earlie hooked her hand through the crook of Kenzie's arm and nodded. They found a spot just under a pair of trees. The ground was damp and began to seep through the blanket immediately.

'Do you want my bag to sit on?' Kenzie asked, but Earlie shook her head. 'Okay. I have some snacks if you want them.' Onto the blanket, Kenzie tossed crisps, a bag of sweets and a couple of apples.

Earlie immediately picked up an apple. She took a large bite of it and her eyes widened almost comically.

'Mmm! How sweet.'

'Yeah—Cripps Pink. My favourite.'

Earlie picked at the waxy pink skin with a nail. 'Are they a delicacy here?'

'Well, they're pretty expensive as apples go.'

Earlie smiled over at Kenzie. 'Where I'm from, gifting someone an apple is a sign of romantic interest.'

'Oh really?' Kenzie said, tilting her head with a smirk. Her heart was beating like a rabbit's but she was determined to play it cool. 'Well there goes my secret.'

When Earlie had finished her apple, eating even the core, she threw what remained into the flooded lake. Sighing, she straightened her legs out on the blanket, pale feet sticking out from the bottom of her dress. Kenzie regarded them with a smile.

'So, do you always wear these kinds of clothes?'

Earlie laughed. 'Of course not. Sometimes I dress up.'

Kenzie raised her eyebrows. 'That's not dressing up?'

Earlie shook her head. 'Look at all this mud.' She lifted a leg, showing Kenzie how it smudged her creamy skin and the hem of her dress.

Kenzie nodded, taking in all the skin bared to her without remorse. 'It's a lovely dress,' she said.

Earlie chuckled. 'If you say so.'

'I do,' Kenzie said earnestly. She was glad Earlie was facing the direction of the water, seemingly in her own little bubble. She couldn't stop looking at her, at the hair that hung as straight and white as paper all the way to the blanket, and the delicate shoulders which could barely hold up the sleeves of her dress. She was having some meddlesome thoughts to boot too, mainly about pushing Earlie back down on said blanket and kissing her senseless.

'How your heart beats,' Earlie whispered from beside her.

Kenzie's gaze sharpened. 'What?'

Smiling, Earlie pulled her knees up and placed her head down on them, facing Kenzie. 'Your heart. It is like a war drum.'

Kenzie frowned, a confused smile on her lips. 'How can you know that?'

'Am I wrong? That your heart beats quicker at thoughts of me?'

Kenzie glanced away, feeling heat come into her cheeks. 'No comment.'

They stayed beside the lake for another forty-five minutes before the water seepage became too much for Kenzie. She gathered her things back into her bag and stood up, reaching a hand down to Earlie.

'I look like I've peed myself,' Kenzie said, running a hand over her sopping chinos.

Earlie giggled. 'Do I?' she asked, executing a twirl. It made the hem of her dress flow around her knees. She raised her willowy arms and fluttered them down like a ballet dancer's. Kenzie's breath caught at the sight. She was one hundred percent sure, in that moment, that she'd never seen anyone more attractive.

Almost without thinking, she reached out and captured Earlie's hand. Earlie stopped spinning, chuckling lightly at something she could see in Kenzie's eyes. She darted closer and with the speed of a lizard's tongue, bestowed a kiss upon Kenzie's lips.

CHAPTER 10

Earlie lay on her side on the bank of the hill, blinking drowsily at the lights winking at her from the valley. At her feet, a fox snuffled noisily. It had been badgering her for about ten minutes now. Earlie gave her toes a little flick.

'Shoo, fox,' she said and the animal bounded away down the hill.

She followed its trail with her eyes, knowing that down there was her sweet little human, tucked up in her bed and dreaming the night away.

Dreaming of her, Earlie hoped.

'Little one.'

Earlie sprang to her feet and whirled. Cerulean was there, grinning. She opened her arms and enveloped Earlie's slight frame, planting a kiss atop her head.

When they parted, Risarial was beside them too, dressed in all the colours of the night. 'Well, you're certainly faring better than I thought you would,' she said, smiling slyly.

Earlie frowned, stepping away from the both of them.

'Ignore her,' Cerulean said. 'Tell me how it's going.'

A smile bloomed on Earlie's face. 'Splendidly. I kissed her. I kissed a mortal.'

Cerulean raised an eyebrow. 'And?'

'And what?'

'And, what was it like?' Cerulean made an impatient gesture. 'Do they kiss like us? How did it feel?'

'It felt nice,' Earlie said, her smile dimming slightly. 'Just

49

nice.'

'What?' Risarial teased. 'No pitter-pattering heartbeat or weakened knees?'

Cerulean frowned, cutting her eyes to Risarial. 'Talking from experience here?'

Risarial ignored her, gaze steady on Earlie who was shaking her head slowly.

'Just softness and warmth,' she said.

Risarial smirked and leaned in close. 'Take it further. You'll feel something then.'

Earlie didn't notice her sisters leaving. The twinkling lights had snared her attention again, along with the slumbering girl who had gifted her an apple.

CHAPTER 11

But Kenzie was not asleep, not even close. She sat at her desk, attention caught between the streetlight-washed road outside her window and the journal lying open in front of her.

She'd written feverishly about her first date with Earlie, detailing everything from the smell of the flooded field to the way Earlie had licked apple juice from her fingers.

Reading it back almost made her question whether it had even happened. Stunning girls—stunning girls interested in *her*—didn't just fall from the sky like Earlie had. If this were any other time in her life, Kenzie reckoned she'd be besieged with doubt. It wasn't that she was down on herself, it was just that this kind of thing simply didn't happen. Not to her. With uni looming just around the corner though, everything about this summer felt surreal and transient.

At the end of their date, as they'd shared another kiss in the woods near the fairy trail, Kenzie discovered that Earlie didn't own a phone. She'd teased her about it for a while before getting serious and figuring out how they were going to stay in contact over the summer.

They eventually decided to leave messages, like lovers of old, near to the tree where they'd first met. It was weird, Kenzie knew, but she was willing to go along with it as long as Earlie was.

She couldn't wait to get down there tomorrow and invite Earlie on another date. She'd already claimed one of her mum's mason jars, the tiny ones she used to store jam samples in, with the red gingham lids. The perfect size to conceal a note in.

Smothering a yawn, Kenzie closed her journal and rose to her feet. She reached out to pull the curtains to just as fox came into view, sniffing around a discarded crisp packet. She paused to watch until it trotted out of sight, and it was another minute until she finally pulled the curtains closed. Why did her street, with the neighbours' bins and mud-dusted cars, look so pretty suddenly?

It was as she was getting into bed that she remembered she hadn't checked her email for university updates. In fact, she hadn't thought of anything uni-related all day.

Snorting softly, she burrowed her face further into her pillow. No need to ask herself what had taken up residence in her mind instead. Beside her, Jenkins rolled onto his back and gave an aggrieved sigh. Reaching out, she gave him a stroke, eventually falling asleep to the memory of Earlie's sweet, apple-flavoured kisses.

CHAPTER 12

Kenzie took her breakfast out into the garden, placing the plate down on the blanket her mum had left out there from the day before. Tucked under her arm were some sheets of her mum's fancy notepaper and the jam jar.

She ate her toast slowly as she thought of what to say. Earlie was always so whimsical in the way she spoke, with all her rhymes and descriptions. She tried, but Kenzie couldn't think up a rhyme to save her life. Deciding the direct approach was best, she put her pen to the paper and wrote:

Hey, really hope you get this and no one else does (so if you are anyone other than Earlie, put this back!!) Just wondered if you did want to pop up to Ackinton? I'd say today but just in case you don't get this until later, maybe tomorrow? Or the day after? As you can see, I'm pretty much free all the time. Looking forward to your reply, feels so weird writing this instead of texting it! Love, Kenzie x

She reread her message a bunch of times before folding it up neatly and pushing it into the jar.

'Wanna help me deliver it?' she asked the dog.

After placing her empty plate into the sink, she picked up a spoon and slipped it into her back pocket. Seemed kind of overkill to bring a spade, and she didn't really want to go digging around with her hands, so she decided a spoon would do.

It took her no time at all to get to the avenue of trees. She slowed down to let another couple walk on ahead and then once they were out of sight, she descended upon the tree. Jenkins, seeing her kneeling down, wandered over and pawed at the ground she was inspecting.

'Move it,' she said, brushing him away.

She found a nice spot just inside a curve at the base of the trunk. The earth there was loamy and easy to manoeuvre with her spoon. She dug a little well a few inches deep before pressing in the jar and covering it back up. The whole thing was over within a minute.

Kenzie sighed, standing up.

'That'll do,' she said to Jenkins.

⇛ ⇝

All day she thought about the note resting there beneath the earth and wondered when it would be best to check on it. Her mum had asked her to help out with the Thursday morning market, affording her with a distraction. She spent a good hour moving chairs and chipped plyboard tables, then setting up her mum's jars of marmalade and chutney. This week, she'd made one from Cripps Pink apples. When her mum wasn't looking, she kept one back, remembering how much Earlie had enjoyed those apples.

She forced herself to wait until dinnertime before heading down to the woods under the guise of taking Jenkins out for a second walk.

Kenzie knew without even seeing a note that Earlie had been there. A ribbon of silk, the same colour as the dress she wore on their date, was wrapped around one of the branches close to the ground.

Some of the earth near it had been disturbed. Kenzie's heart thumped with excitement. Without checking to see if anyone was watching, she knelt down and began digging. She'd forgotten her spoon this time but she didn't care.

Her nails were black by the time she found the tiny bottle. She held it up to eyelevel. It was small enough to be held between her forefinger and thumb, made up in frosted purple glass and stuffed with a cork. Inside, she could see a tightly-coiled slip of paper.

It took a while to dig the cork out with her lack of nails. When she had, she upended the bottle so the paper fell into the well of her palm. Sitting down upon a bough, Kenzie unravelled it.

I would dearly love that, the note read. *On Freya's day at the eleventh hour, I will be under the arch of the two swans. Meet me there. Yours, Earlie.*

Kenzie grinned. She knew exactly what Earlie meant this time. Freya's day—Friday—named after the goddess of fertility and love. How apt, Kenzie thought. Eleventh hour was easy enough and the arch Earlie referred to was one she often walked under on her canal walks with Jenkins.

Feeling buzzed, Kenzie slipped the bottle into her pocket and jogged all the way back through the woods to the house.

CHAPTER 13

In the mornings, when the sky was hazy and the grass still dewy, Earlie would walk through meadows and along riverbanks and sit in the fields with the cows and sheep. When the farmers came, she'd hold herself still, gathering her glamour tightly around her until the men, faces work-worn and clothes muddied, drove out of the gates and left her alone with their animals again.

Come afternoon, Earlie would take herself off to sleep in the soft loam beneath hedges, fieldmice and spiders coming to nest in her hair, taking a break from the toils of the day. It was there in her safe hiding spaces that she would think about her mortal, about her chapped lips and soft, yielding body.

She wasn't sure if love was a choice. Risarial said it wasn't, that it was more like something that happened upon you unexpectantly, most often uninvited, like the sudden thrust of a venomous snakes' neck.

But when Earlie first saw Kenzie on that trail, her flushed face and tiny, brown freckles, it was her she had chosen, right in that moment.

It was only when night fell that Earlie drifted down the hills and into the humans' town to spy on the creatures who dwelled there.

Earthside was such a strange realm, almost stranger than the humans who called it home. The season was so hot, something she attributed to being the cause of their much sun-reddened and wrinkled faces, the bruising beneath their eyes and the blemishes which littered their skin. Their houses also reminded Earlie of blemishes, the way they protruded from the soil, each so different from their neighbours'.

Unsightly as they were, Earlie found she couldn't stay away.

On one particular night, she stood in the middle of a garden of such a home, a brook loud at her back, staring into the orange, steamy windows, where a family sat around a table.

They weren't eating. The kids were restless, getting up and leaving the room, only to return to their seats a moment later, something new in hand to entertain them. A young girl with red curls held a naked doll. A boy, slightly older, thrust his plastic dinosaur at it, making the girl's face contour in outrage. The parents barely looked their way, only the mother reaching out a hand to silence them. They had a bottle of wine sitting between them, the red liquid glowing deeply under the stylish hanging lights.

Though Earlie stared, she couldn't tell if this family were happy or not. Risarial had been right. Humans were complicated.

'Are you Patricia?'

Earlie turned from the window. A boy of about ten stood behind her, balancing a plastic water gun on his shoulder. He was wearing blue pyjamas with footballs printed all over them and he watched her curiously, a tiny frown between his eyes.

'Who is Patricia?'

The boy shot a quick look back at the house. 'The lady my dad sees.' The boy's voice was quieter now, less certain. 'I'm not supposed to tell anyone. I wasn't supposed to see.'

Earlie thought of her father and his endless march of consorts, all with their long, luscious hair and nimble, harp-plucking fingers. Unlike the boy's mother, Earlie's couldn't care less. 'I am not she.'

'Oh.' The boy glared. 'Another one then?' Emitting a small grunt of displeasure, he raised his gun and shot a line of water at Earlie's stomach.

Earlie looked down at the patch of wet spreading on her dress then back up at the boy. Sensing he might have made a mistake, he began backing away but Earlie snared him, wrapping him up in her glamour. She smiled at the way his eyes widened in the dark. Such tiny, button eyes. Hard to stick a pin through. Held immobile, the boy couldn't scream. He could only squirm and hit out at her with his water gun.

Holding him still in her arms, Earlie bowed her head and said into his ear, 'Men like your father need their consorts, youngling. It softens the rage in their hearts.'

Earlie dropped her arms and the boy fell to the ground. Scrambling to his feet, he ran towards the patio doors. 'There's a girl in the garden!' he shouted. 'There's a girl!'

Earlie turned and melted back into the shadows. When the family came to the window, there was nothing out there to see but the water gun lying forgotten in the grass.

CHAPTER 14

Earlie waited for her on the narrow towpath beneath the bridge, staring down into the water speckled with fallen leaves. Her bare toes rested over the lip of the path, inches from the canal.

'Hey,' Kenzie said hushedly, not wanting to spook her. Earlie turned. 'Don't you ever wear shoes?'

Earlie only smiled and let herself be pulled in for a kiss.

'You look good,' Kenzie whispered.

'I have been thinking about you,' Earlie replied.

'Oh yeah? Thinking about what?'

Kenzie took her hand and they started along the canal.

'I was wondering if you'd like to spend the night with me.' Earlie glanced up at her, mouth slightly parted as she waited for Kenzie's answer.

'Oh.' Kenzie's skin flushed all over. 'Yeah sure, I'd love that.'

Earlie squeezed her hand and smiled.

The walk from Kirkall Bridge to Ackinton was about an hour along the canal path. Between the shadowy tunnels and bridges, and high banks of shrubbery and wildflowers, were open meadows and the back gardens of the more affluent houses in the area.

Kenzie watched Earlie take it all in—the waving tree tops and passing ducks, and even the people who brushed passed them on the path seemed to be a marvel to her. It probably made the pair of them look like a couple of hardcore tourists but it was kind of nice for Kenzie to look at her hometown through newer eyes.

About forty minutes in, they reached the abandoned mill where Ackinton moored their narrowboats. It was a pretty dodgy boater community, different to the one nearer to Kirkall Bridge where the banks had been cultivated into little gardens and the residents drank tea on their decks in the sun.

Here, some of the boats looked like they'd been bobbing there since the beginning of time, rusted with smashed in windows, and the occupants were generally made up of brawny men and greasy-haired girls who smoked weed and glared at passers-by.

Almost without thinking, Kenzie reached out and wrapped an arm around Earlie's shoulders, tugging her close.

Earlie pulled her gaze away from the water. 'What are you doing?'

'Protecting you from the scary men,' Kenzie grinned.

'Just like Cerulean!' Earlie sighed and shook her head.

'Are you the baby then?'

'I am the youngest daughter of Adelina and Folred. Risarial is their oldest and enjoys lording it.'

'Such interesting names,' Kenzie said. 'You definitely wouldn't find them on a keyring in the visitor centre.'

'There are ten Folred's in our community. Father was the first.'

'When you say community, what do you mean exactly?' Kenzie asked. 'Is it like a hippie commune or a religious thing?'

'Religion,' Earlie mused, clicking her tongue. 'Do you ever think that those gods you worship are perhaps below the Earth instead of above it?'

'What do you mean? Wait, are you Satanists?' Kenzie asked, whirling round. 'No shade if you are. I know it's on the rise and stands for some good stuff—you know, like feminism and freedom.'

Earlie laughed, a tittering sound which made Kenzie smile. 'Oh Kenzie. Funny, lovely Kenzie. We have no religion. Not anymore.'

'Ah. Okay. I won't ask anymore.'

They eventually arrived in Ackinton, emerging into the deserted market which stood in the shadows of the valley's viaduct. Earlie looked up just as a train rolled past.

'Are you hungry?' Kenzie asked.

'I've yet to find food today.'

'Well, we're gonna sort that out.' Kenzie steered them in the direction of the high street. 'There's a café my friend told me about that opened recently. It's supposed to be pretty nice. Let's see if we can find it and have an early lunch.'

Ackinton's high street was less busy than Kirkall's and was formed more of locals than tourists. A mother with one child, and another in a pushchair, rushed passed, hand firmly clamped around the toddlers' who was screaming, her angry face red and wet. As her eyes spotted Earlie, she stopped abruptly and gawked as she passed, fingers now firmly in her mouth.

'Made a friend,' Kenzie commented.

Earlie smiled. 'Clever youngling, with the Sight.'

Kenzie opened her mouth to query that but when Earlie looked at her, her smile now dimmer but still there, she found her thoughts whisked away as if on a wind. She turned back to the storefronts they were passing, running her eyes over the old tarnished stone and hand-painted signs.

Though it wasn't as well-to-do, Ackinton was still home to some cool independent art galleries and vintage book and record shops. Earlie, still holding onto Kenzie's hand, pulled as she peered into the windows.

'We can go in some if you like,' Kenzie said.

Without a word, Earlie stepped into the nearest shop. It was a cluttered bric-a-brac place which smelt of wood varnish and must. The shop owner, half-hidden behind a box of photo frames, nodded at them.

'Smells of history,' Earlie said, nose raised.

Kenzie nodded. 'My mum's pretty keen on this sort of stuff. She's a bit of a hoarder.'

Past all the cabinets and old books and shelves of creepy-looking teddies was a mini art gallery. Earlie stood in the centre of the only uncluttered space in the shop and did a slow turn before stepping up to one painting. It was a large landscape depicting some kind of gathering in the woods. There was fire and dancing and people with faces of rapture. Kenzie glanced at the label. *An Assembly of Faeries, Lucelia Irvine.*

'You wouldn't look out of place in that,' Kenzie said, wrapping her arms around Earlie from behind.

'I'd like to take you with me.'

Kenzie chuckled. 'Now, I think I would look out of place.'

Earlie turned in Kenzie's arms. She pressed their lips together and kept them there until Kenzie began to forget where they were. Only when Earlie's stomach growled did they part.

'You need food,' Kenzie said pointedly. 'Come on.'

Without protest, Earlie let herself be led from the shop.

They were seated on a narrow, outdoor terrace which overlooked the canal. It was quiet here, the terrace bracketed by the backs of all the other shops and private flats. A few buildings down, a woman read on a balcony, her bare legs propped up on the railing's edge. At the lip of the canal, a father and his young daughter fed the geese, the water dotted with hunks of bread the girl liberally threw down. Kenzie could hear her excited squeals from where she sat.

She turned back to her menu. 'Have an idea of what you're getting?'

Earlie was running a fingertip along all the options, her face still in concentration. After a moment, her finger halted and she jabbed at the laminated sheet. Kenzie leaned over to read.

'*Citrus, pomegranate and bulgur wheat salad.* Hm. Healthy. Think I'm gonna go for a wrap myself.'

When the waitress returned with their drinks, Kenzie rattled off their orders then began pouring from the pitcher of mint and cucumber water. She pushed one towards Earlie, who inspected it before bringing it to her lips.

'The water tastes so strange here,' Earlie said, lowering her glass.

'Does it? The water's soft up here. Maybe it's hard where you're from or something.' Kenzie took a sip, swilling it around her mouth. 'Tastes fine to me but I guess I'm used to it.'

Earlie regarded her for a moment. 'Do you think that you'll stay here forever?' she asked, running a finger around the rim of her glass.

'In Kirkall you mean?'

'Just here.'

'Well, I'm off to Manchester soon, aren't I?' Kenzie shrugged. 'I've heard they have a pretty high retention rate. Maybe I'll stay there if I like it. I can't see myself living in Kirkall forever, to be honest.'

Earlie nodded haltingly, as if that wasn't quite the correct answer, or Kenzie had answered the wrong question.

'What about you?' Kenzie asked. 'What are your future plans?'

'The future doesn't exist,' Earlie said, gaze drifting back to the water below. 'There is only the present, and the present is all there ever will be.'

Kenzie grinned. 'I like that. I'm all for making the most of the moment.'

Earlie smiled, tilting her head. 'You are, aren't you?'

Before Kenzie could reply, the waitress arrived with their food. Kenzie pointed the salad towards Earlie before accepting her own plate.

'That looks good,' she said, nodding towards Earlie's salad. It was a bright, colourful arrangement, the pomegranate seeds glistening in the sun.

Earlie picked up the plate and held it under her nose. 'Mm. Smells divine.'

Kenzie glanced at her own side salad, drooping against her wrap. She knew she wouldn't touch it.

'Hey, feel free to take a bite of mine if you want,' she said to Earlie. 'I haven't touched that second wrap yet.'

'What is inside?'

Kenzie prized her wrap open slightly. 'Um, chicken, chilli sauce and some other stuff.'

'Chicken?' Earlie asked, zeroing in on Kenzie's food.

'Yeah…' Kenzie trailed off at the look on Earlie's face. 'Oh shit, you're a vegan aren't you?' Earlie cut her eyes to Kenzie's. They were strangely cold. 'I should have asked.' She reached out and covered one of Earlie's hands. 'Does it bother you if I eat this?'

'Does it not bother you?'

Kenzie pursed her lips. 'No, not really. It's just what I've been brought up on.'

Earlie removed her hand from Kenzie's. She picked up a slice of orange and nibbled it in silence.

The girl who was feeding the geese suddenly shrieked when one raised its wings and hissed at her. Kenzie was glad to see a smile come back to Earlie's face.

'Mean things, those,' she said. 'Jenkins has been pecked a few times.'

'Silly wolf,' Earlie tittered. Still looking at the bird, she said, 'Where I'm from, an encounter with a goose like that can mean your life is about to take an abrupt turn.'

'Oh really?'

Earlie nodded. 'The Goose; The Navigator.'

'That's cool. And kind of fitting.' Kenzie let out a sigh. 'Things be changing recently.'

'In a way which makes you glad?'

'Very glad.'

Earlie looked pleased. She picked up a pomegranate seed and bit into it with her two front teeth. Kenzie didn't think she'd ever seen someone with such tiny, perfect teeth. When Earlie's tongue peeked out, swiping at the juice on her lips, Kenzie had to take a bite of her wrap to distract herself from her sudden lascivious thoughts.

'Have you ever shared your body with someone, Kenzie?' Earlie asked, almost as if she had read her mind.

Kenzie stopped chewing. 'Yeah, 'course,' she said, swallowing her mouthful. 'Couple of people. You?'

Earlie smiled and dipped her head slightly. Usually her smiles were sweet and light; this one looked cunning. 'A couple.'

Kenzie picked up her serviette, wringing it between her fingers. 'We don't have to…we can do it when you want, you know. We don't have to rush or anything.'

Earlie frowned. 'Rush what?'

Kenzie smiled uneasily. 'Never mind. Just want to make sure you're into this, that's all.'

'I am. You intrigue me endlessly, Kenzie.'

Kenzie chuckled. 'Wow. You really do have a way with words, you know that?'

In lieu of an answer, Earlie lifted her foot beneath the table and ran it up Kenzie's leg. It was all Kenzie could do, after that, to calmly finish her meal and signal for the bill.

❦

They were quiet on their way back to the canal path. Even Kenzie, who knew she had a tendency to prattle on, couldn't find any words to speak. The silence surrounding them was both delicate and heavy. Earlie held Kenzie's hand tightly and Kenzie found it difficult, every time they passed beneath a bridge, not to spin Earlie towards her and push her back against the cold wall of the archways.

The next bridge they came upon, when Earlie dropped

her hand and ran her fingers up the sensitive skin of Kenzie's inner arm, she didn't stop herself. She heard Earlie gasp in surprise but she smothered it with a kiss, manoeuvring her gently against the sloping wall.

'Been wanting to do that for a while,' she whispered when they parted.

Earlie looked up at her with her huge, searching eyes, a smile threatening to bloom on her lips. She took a breath to speak when a throat clearing sounded from beside them.

Kenzie looked up, stepping away from Earlie as two men appeared from around the wall. They looked them over with toothy smiles, the way they paid closer attention to Earlie immediately making Kenzie's skin crawl.

'Sorry to interrupt, *ladies*,' one of them said. He was the skinniest of the two, with a face of shabby stubble and an eyebrow ring which looked infected. 'Just wondered if we could join in, you know?'

'Piss off,' Kenzie said, reaching out for Earlie's hand.

'Don't think we will,' a second man said. He was stockier, face more serious. 'You're on our bit of path.' He pointed behind him, where a ratty narrowboat was idling. 'We live here, yeah, and we don't want to have to look up and see two dykes going at it.'

'Alright, we'll go,' Kenzie said. She kept her voice low but it was hard to keep the edge of fear and anger from it.

'Nah, nah, nah.' The first man held up both palms. 'We don't want you to leave.' He glanced at Earlie. 'Especially not this one.'

'Yeah, you can sling it. Leave this one here.' The second man reached out and touched the material of Earlie's dress. Earlie made a sound of protest and swiped at him.

'*Ooh*,' the man mocked, holding his hands up like a boxers'. 'Feisty.'

'Let's just go back,' Kenzie said, turning Earlie around.

'Ah, ah, ah, I don't think so.'

The skinny man rounded them quickly, pulling Kenzie up short. She looked behind her. The other man standing there raised his chin, face devoid of emotion. Kenzie swallowed convulsively, heart racing. They were trapped. She glanced at the water. At the moment, it was their only option.

'What do you want?' she asked. If she could keep the men talking for long enough, someone was surely bound to come across them.

The skinny man let out a low whistle, as if he was seriously contemplating her question. His eyes ran up and down Earlie's body then he looked at Kenzie and said, 'Her.'

Lurching forward, he caught Earlie by the tops of her arms. Earlie called out, kicking at him.

'Let me go you great oaf!' she shrieked.

The man laughed. 'You hearing this, Daryl?'

But Daryl wasn't joining in. He was pensive, looking around him. 'Come on, move her quick,' he said.

'Fuck off!' Kenzie curled a fist and brought it down hard on one of the arms that held Earlie.

The man's face twisted. He reached a leg out and kicked her. 'Piss off you dyke bitch!'

The kick wasn't hard enough to cause any damage but it took Kenzie by surprise and she fell, almost toppling into the canal. Daryl loomed over, his face now as ugly as the other man's. He spat a trail of saliva at her and disappeared around the arch where Earlie had been taken.

Kenzie jumped to her feet and followed. The stocky man had Earlie pressed up against the dirty, mossy wall, his face close to hers. Kenzie looked behind her. The canal path was hidden now but she still opened her mouth and yelled, 'Help!'

Daryl slapped a hand over her mouth. 'Shut up,' he said with gritted teeth. He pulled her back against his body and she closed her eyes at the disgust that washed over her. When his hands began wandering, she opened them again and looked into Earlie's.

She was staring back at her, face strangely passive. She closed her eyes and leaned her head back against the wall, curling a hand around the back of the man's head. She put her lips to his ear. Kenzie couldn't hear what she said but the man paused then raised his head. Earlie looked into his eyes and Kenzie saw her nod her head just slightly. The man pushed off her. He took a step back and then another, and then he was off stumbling down the bank and into a thicket of trees until Kenzie couldn't see him anymore.

'Aiden?' Daryl called after him. 'Aiden, where the fuck you going man?'

Daryl let her go. Kenzie leaped away and came to Earlie's side, grasping her arm. She made sure the men were well and truly gone before turning her attention to Earlie.

'Shit, are you alright?' she said, pulling her back onto the towpath.

Earlie nodded jerkily and Kenzie could see that she was shaking. 'Hey, come here.' She pulled Earlie into a hug, her heart falling at how she trembled against her. 'Hey, it's okay now,' she whispered, barely able to see the shapes of the men now, crossing the field on the other side of the thicket. 'They're gone now. You don't have to be scared.'

'I am not scared. I am furious.' Earlie pulled out of Kenzie's arms. Her eyes were wild. 'Disgusting, vile, swamp-dwelling creatures,' she whispered brokenly.

Kenzie reached out to stroke Earlie's shoulder. 'What did you say to get him to stop?'

'I told him to keep going until he fell off a cliff.' Earlie let out a shrill laugh. 'He will walk and walk and walk. Maybe days, maybe weeks. All the way to death.'

Kenzie looked at Earlie. Could she be in shock? She was always pale, but now she was practically deathly apart from the two points of colour in her cheeks.

'We should probably get off this path,' Kenzie said. 'I don't want anyone else getting the same idea.'

'Oh Kenzie, I feel like I might explode.' Earlie turned away and walked a couple of steps, her fingers fluttering spasmodically at her sides. It was an action her mum sometimes did to stave off her occasional panic attacks.

'Earlie, this way.'

Earlie turned back to her but instead of following her down the path, she lifted her arms into a dive and jumped into the canal.

'Dude!'

Earlie surfaced slowly, hair plastered to her face and concealing her eyes like some malevolent, water-dwelling creature.

'That canal is not clean,' Kenzie told her. 'It's full of duck shit and all sorts.'

Earlie raised a hand and weaved it through the water. 'You are right,' she said, flicking the water away. 'Dirty and polluted. Like much of your world, it seems to me.'

But instead of getting out, Earlie began a slow breaststroke down the canal.

'You'll get sick,' Kenzie said, keeping pace with her. 'Please get out.'

Earlie rolled onto her back, lazily cartwheeling her arms on top of the water like she was making a snow-angel. Despite her agitation, Kenzie found the sight strangely Ophelia-esque.

'Oh, Kenzie,' Earlie breathed. 'I feel so much better. How the water soothes.'

'Cool, come out now then.'

By this time, Earlie had reached the first of the moored barges. She rightened herself in the water and regarded the closest to her curiously.

'Gold Aurora.' She ran a finger over the chipped blue paint. 'How pretty.'

She looked up, peering over the edge of it before grasping the gunwale and pulling herself over and onto the bow.

'Earlie!' Kenzie hissed. 'What are you doing?'

'There's no one in it,' Earlie said, walking around the tiny deck. It was crammed with pots of wilting flowers. 'The vessel is empty.'

'Oh, bloody hell.' Kenzie peered around. She couldn't

see anyone else, not on the canal path or in any of the boats, but it didn't mean people weren't around.

'You're off your rocker, you are,' she said, unable to help the exasperated smile on her lips.

Earlie reached down and snapped the stem of a camomile flower. Wading to the edge of the deck, she presented it to Kenzie.

'Very nice, thank you. Now come on.' She reached out and pulled Earlie onto the path. The scent of dank water clung to her and her hair was dotted with duckweed. Kenzie pulled some of the wet strands out of her face. 'You're gonna need a shower,' she said, taking hold of Earlie's hand. 'Come on. We'll go to mine.'

CHAPTER 15

Kenzie sat on the sofa with her legs stretched out, idly watching some cookery show on the telly. The chef sliced into a raw chicken carcass and Kenzie smiled briefly, thinking she was glad Earlie wasn't here to see that. In the kitchen, she heard the slamming of the washing machine door and the tap running. Her mum was in there, tending to Earlie's sodden dress.

'Oi,' she called. 'What's your friend's name again?'

'Earlie.'

'Earlie?' Her mum came into the living room, a pile of folded towels in her arms. 'That's an odd one. Pretty though, I suppose.'

Kenzie nodded. The thought that Earlie was right now naked in her shower was even prettier.

'And how did you two meet?'

'On the fairy trail,' Kenzie said. 'Kind of. Then she turned up at the campout the other night.'

'Hm.' Her mum offered no further comment than that.

When Earlie came down the stairs fifteen minutes later, she was dressed in one of Kenzie's baggiest tees. It hung off her shoulders and stopped at just above her knees.

'Hey,' Kenzie said, eyes rivetted to the sight.

Earlie looked at her and frowned, then pulled one of the arms further down her shoulder. The skin there was dotted pink. 'I've been marred.'

'Oh dear,' Kenzie's mum said, taking in the angry hives.

'Water too hot?'

'No.'

'Might be those chemicals they put in the water then, love. You're probably sensitive.'

Earlie scratched at herself. 'Itches.'

'Go get her some E45,' Kenzie's mum said, nodding the two of them up the stairs.

Kenzie got off the sofa and guided Earlie out of the room. 'My room's just up here. I'll get the cream from the bathroom.'

When Kenzie entered her room, tub of cream in hand, Earlie was sat at the very foot of her bed, looking up at her expectantly.

'Is it all over?' Kenzie asked.

'Mostly my shoulders and legs.'

Kenzie nodded, scooping a little cream into her palm. She started with Earlie's bared shoulder.

'How are you doing?' she asked as she worked. 'You know, after what happened.'

'It is all but forgotten.'

Kenzie glanced up. Earlie was staring fixedly out of the window, face serene.

'That shoulder's done.' Kenzie moved onto the other, gently pulling the t-shirt down. 'Has this happened before?'

'No.'

'Hm. Wonder what's up with that then.' When she was finished with that, she glanced at Earlie's legs. 'Do you want me to do your legs? Looks like they're fading already.'

Earlie parted her legs slightly, baring to Kenzie the rashes along her inner thighs. 'Not really.'

'Alright,' Kenzie murmured, heart beginning to thump. As she knelt, she wondered briefly if Earlie was playing with her. It was always so hard to tell.

She scooped up more cream and started with Earlie's left leg. There were no marks on her calves but Kenzie administered to them anyway, feeling strangely shy to venture any higher. Soon, she had reached her knee, her fingers fluttering over Earlie's thigh. When she accidently brushed the inside of it, Earlie let out a little trickle of breath.

'Do you want me to keep going?' Kenzie whispered.

Wordlessly, Earlie nodded.

Kenzie pulled her hands away and put them to Earlie's hips instead. She raised her head and kissed Earlie's lips, gently at first, then harder when Earlie put her palms to her cheeks.

'Hang on.' With some effort, Kenzie pulled away. 'I'm just going to wash my hands. I don't want to…touch you, with all this on them.'

Earlie's arms fell away from her. Jogging to the bathroom on the other side of the landing, Kenzie quickly rinsed her hands. She dried them more slowly, thinking about the girl currently waiting for her in her bed. Was this really about to happen? She wanted it to, she really did, but she was also nervous and a bit overwhelmed. Determined not to show it, Kenzie steeled herself before returning to her room.

Earlie had removed her t-shirt. She wore nothing, standing there casually in the middle of Kenzie's rug. Kenzie's breath caught. She leaned back on the door until it closed with a click. Then she pushed off it and walked over to Earlie who immediately wrapped her arms around Kenzie's neck.

'Wait,' Kenzie said. 'Let me close the curtains.'

Shut to the sun, the murky light of her bedroom rendered Earlie even more stunning, the shadows softening the plains of her body and bringing to light her waxen complexion. Kenzie stepped back up to her; she was almost too much to look at.

They kissed slowly, reverently. A minute of that and Kenzie's breathing was almost embarrassingly heavy. Earlie's remained calm and steady, even her heart, when Kenzie put a palm to her chest, beat at half the speed of hers. At her touch, Earlie pulled back and twisted her fingers into the material of Kenzie's shirt.

'Remove all this,' she commanded.

Kenzie reached for the buttons of her shirt, then her shorts. In a matter of seconds, she was just as bare as Earlie.

'What a beautiful, bountiful body you have,' Earlie said, running her eyes over all the curves and dips of Kenzie's torso.

Kenzie chuckled breathlessly. 'No one's ever said that before.'

'Like a ripe apple,' Earlie continued. She reached out and ran her fingertips over Kenzie's stomach. 'A peach about to burst.'

Almost abruptly, Earlie pulled away and walked over to the bed. She lay back on it and beckoned Kenzie over with her eyes.

When Kenzie climbed over her, she said, 'We have to be quiet, alright. Mum's only downstairs.'

Earlie didn't answer, only raised her legs, wrapping them around Kenzie's waist and pulling her face back down to hers. Kenzie fanned her hands around Earlie's shoulders before moving them lower and—

'Kenz?'

Kenzie wrenched her mouth away at the sound of her mum calling up the stairs. She held her breath, waiting to hear her heavy footsteps over the sound of her beating heart. After a moment of hearing nothing, she shouted back, 'Yeah?'

'I'm just popping to Sandra's for a coffee.' Kenzie heard the metallic clink of keys and the zip of a bag. 'Reckon I'll be a couple of hours. That alright?'

Kenzie put a hand over her eyes. 'Yeah, sure,' she said, hoping her voice sounded normal. 'See you in a bit.' The front door shut. Kenzie removed her hand and smiled. 'That was close.'

Earlie didn't smile back. Her eyes were at half-slit, mouth parted, drawing in breaths which were finally quickening. The look froze Kenzie to the spot.

'Kenzie,' Earlie breathed. 'You have to touch me now.'

❧ ❧

Kenzie barely heard her mum returning. It was more than two hours later—more like four—and judging by the sound of her singing downstairs, she'd had more than just a coffee with Sandra.

Kenzie didn't care, she didn't care about anything in that moment. After Earlie had left, she spent an interminable amount of time just lying on her bed, looking up at the glow-in-the-dark stars she'd had tacked to her ceiling since she was a kid, and reliving the past few hours in her mind.

Earlie wasn't at all what Kenzie had expected. She was always so poised and quiet and Kenzie expected her to be the same in bed but she wasn't like that at all, not when things had really got going. She was—well—bouncy was the first word that came to mind. Kenzie smiled; that had surprised her. Whenever she thought she had her opinion of Earlie down, she went and did something to completely upend it.

When she finally dragged herself from the bed, it was only to go sit at her desk and rehash the event in her diary. This time, after she'd finished, she placed the book right at the back of the desk drawer, beneath some other notebooks, just in case her mum got into one of her snooping moods.

She felt an almost overwhelming urge to text Asa, to let him know this big, massive thing going on in her usually quiet life. It had been fun for a while, keeping everything a secret but now it felt like something had changed, intensified, and she might go out of her mind if she didn't tell someone.

She decided to call him instead. Too much had happened to cram into a message. As she listened to the dial tone, Kenzie wondered where Earlie was and if she was thinking about her, too.

CHAPTER 16

Earlie lay back on the tomb, the cold stone of it cooling her overheated skin. An ocean of stars stretched out above her, the moon a lighthouse in the middle of it all. Though its light was brilliant, the scuffs and craters on its surface sharp, Earlie saw it all through a wavy film, her mind half there and half with the girl whose bed she had shared just hours before.

Earlie sighed and turned so that she was lying on her stomach. Eyes half open, she saw the embossed face of the mortal's grave she was lying on only millimetres from her own. Leaning down, she kissed the chipped, stone lips.

'You humans are so beautiful,' she whispered.

'I think her mind has run away.'

Earlie smiled at the voice. Cerulean sat perched on a gravestone a few paces away, a leafy branch in her hand from which she plucked cherries to place into her mouth.

'I think it's rather her body,' Risarial replied, standing tall amidst the sea of grave markers. She had on a dark shirt, the ribbed material of it riding all the way up her neck. It wasn't of fae design; Earlie wondered if she'd found it on one of her earthly travels.

Risarial drifted closer. 'Am I right, sister?'

Earlie pulled herself into a sitting position. 'I feel dirty and exquisitely clean all at once.'

'When was the last time you bathed?' Cerulean asked her, tossing her stripped branch away. 'You smell like a dank swamp.'

Earlie's smile fell. 'I bathed just today.'

'Might I smuggle you some rose water?'

'No,' Earlie said, face creasing into a frown. 'And stop visiting me. You're meddling.'

Cerulean raised both her palms. 'Just checking up on you.' She grinned devilishly. 'Earthside is full of dangers, you know.'

'She's right,' Risarial said. She had her head tilted, regarding Earlie with a look which was at once both maternal and scheming. 'Dangers of the heart being the most insidious of them all.'

'I am in no danger.'

'I believe you,' said Cerulean. She pointed at Earlie accusingly. 'You deflowered your mortal. I know it. You hold the same gleam in your eye as you did after seducing that poor seelie kobold. They're still looking for him, in the court, did you know?'

Earlie flicked her hair over her shoulders. A small black spider, disturbed by the movement, clawed frantically at the strands with its legs. 'And what of it?'

'Come now, no need to be coy,' Risarial said. She folded her arms. 'It is what we are here to do, is it not?'

Earlie lost her uppishness. She worried her bottom lip for a moment before saying, 'They get awfully hot and bothered, don't they?'

Risarial tipped her head back and laughed softly.

Cerulean looked between their shared smiles. 'I feel like a stranger to this party all of a sudden.'

'You'll get your turn,' Risarial said. She turned back to Earlie. 'You can come back now.'

'I don't want to.' Earlie crawled backwards, taking refuge in the cold arms of the tomb. 'I'm not ready.'

'Maybe not tonight,' Risarial acquiesced quietly, firmly. 'But soon.'

Earlie nodded once. 'Soon.'

CHAPTER 17

The storms finally fell the day after, commencing with an afternoon thunderstorm of the likes Kirkall Bridge hadn't seen in a long time. There were dangers of flooding, down on the edges of the canal where the larger houses sat. The field which housed the skatepark was already flooded, water pooling at the bottom of the ramps, pissing off the kids who usually played there. It didn't stop them though, only increased their chances of accidents.

Kenzie still checked the tree for new messages every day, soaking herself to the skin in the deluges, enjoying the mulchy smell of the hot, wet earth. Though she had left new messages, she hadn't received any herself for days.

On the third day, when twin rainbows arced over the whitening skies, Kenzie unearthed a new note. Her heart flooded with relief so heavy it startled her. She hadn't wanted to admit to herself how worried she'd been that Earlie had ended her holiday prematurely. She knew the day was coming, and soon, but not today, please not today.

Meet me at the top on the morrow, the point of two coins, the wall between our homes. I lie on the bench at mid-morn, hungry for your touch.

Though Kenzie's pulse quickened at the words, she forced herself to focus. This was the most abstract yet. Somewhere with a bench, somewhere high—the rest she didn't get.

She tucked the note away for now. It was only morning; she had all day to figure it out.

⇜ ⇝

Going for afternoon tea at Wendy's Teahouse was something Kenzie and her mum tried to do bi-monthly. It wasn't really her scene, all that florally bone china and lace, but the cakes and sandwiches were second to none. It also didn't hurt that the owners, who she'd known all her life, always sneaked them a freebie—usually a new tart they were concocting or a sandwich combo.

This afternoon they sat beside the patio doors which stood open to the small garden at the back. The day was blustery and overcast but there was no further rain forecasted for the rest of the week, to Kenzie's relief. She wanted to be out in the wild with Earlie.

'You alright, love?'

Kenzie pulled her gaze away from the garden. 'Huh?'

'You look a million miles away there,' her mum replied. She pulled Kenzie's teacup closer and poured from the pot.

Kenzie sat up straighter and pulled her chair closer to the table. 'Sorry. Bit distracted.'

'Why's that then? And get tucked into these sandwiches, please.'

Kenzie began shaking her head, paused, then reached into her pocket and pulled out Earlie's note. 'That girl,' she began. 'The one who was round the other day. Earlie. She wants to meet me tomorrow. We leave notes like this because she doesn't have a phone.' Kenzie pushed the note across the table. 'She likes doing these riddles, but I can't work this one out.' Hastily, she added, 'Just don't read the last bit.'

Kenzie's mum picked up the note curiously. 'Bit odd, isn't it?'

Kenzie shrugged. 'It's kind of fun.'

Her mum read the note then tutted, glancing up at her.

'Don't read the last bit, she says.'

Kenzie smiled apologetically.

'*Meet me at the top on the 'morrow, the point of two coins…*' her mum murmured. 'Well, it's got to be Salkings Hill, hasn't it? That's the only thing that springs to mind. Don't get the 'between our homes' bit, though.'

Kenzie snatched the note back, reading it again. 'Yeah! That's got to be it.' She slapped herself on the forehead. 'Duh. The homes bit is because she lives up north, I think. So the hill overlooks here and then the hills a bit more north. Maybe. I reckon so anyway.'

'Well, there you go,' her mum said, bringing her teacup to her mouth. She nodded towards the cake stand between them. 'Now please, eat these sandwiches.'

CHAPTER 18

Mid-morning for Kenzie was ten o'clock; she hoped it was for Earlie too. The trek up Salkings Hill had her breathless and sweating by the time she'd reached the top, wet grass soaking through her shoes and sticking to their sides.

As she'd promised, Earlie was sitting on the bench there. She had on a white dress today, almost as sheer as the one Kenzie had seen her in the very first time they had met. This one fell to her shins, an ornate lace trim caressing the skin there.

'You kinda look like a ghost, sitting there,' Kenzie said with a smile. Earlie sprang up and kissed her. 'You're lucky I'm here at all; your note was tricky.'

Earlie smiled. 'I knew you would be here.'

Earlie drifted away, walking along the crest of the hill. Kenzie followed, finally able to enjoy the view now that her breathing had levelled out. One side of the hill, where the bench faced, sloped all the way back to the town, which glistened in the sun in the nest of the valley. The other showed the wild countryside, with its dry moors and sheep and craggy hillsides. Earlie spent a long time facing that way, gaze rapt on Harmon Blythe's fairy hill. There was a hint of a smile on her lips and she looked so at peace, it made Kenzie's heart clench.

'Nice view, isn't it?' Kenzie asked, placing her hands on Earlie's hips from behind.

'The very best,' Earlie replied, interlocking their fingers.

They came to rest at the foot of the bench where Kenzie spread out a blanket—plastic backed this time. The long grasses in front of them were flooded from the recent rains, forming a little pond. It wasn't as magical as Earlie's field; long, spindly briars stretched their fingers into the water and leaves, black and rotten, clogged the edges of it.

When Kenzie sat down, Earlie came to lie between her outstretched legs, leaning back against her body. Kenzie closed her eyes and ran her lips over Earlie's white shoulder, breathing in her smell. Always floral, with a hint of soil.

'You smell like wild things,' she whispered.

Earlie turned her head and Kenzie pressed her lips there, first to her cheek, then to the corner of her mouth, before kissing her properly. She spread her palms and squeezed gently at the soft skin around Earlie's hips, something that made her rear up against her, something that Kenzie wanted to repeat again and again.

Earlie pulled away, leaving Kenzie looking into the depthless irises of her too-blue eyes. She was about to comment on them when a scream rent the air—animalistic and terrified.

Kenzie whipped her head round, heart pounding at the suddenness of it. Beside the pond, a baby rabbit was being pursued by a stoat. The stoat had its mouth around the scruff of the rabbit's neck, who threw its body around, desperately trying to dislodge its pursuer.

'Shit,' Kenzie muttered, hurriedly extricating herself from Earlie.

'Don't,' Earlie breathed into her ear, tightening her grip on her. 'Leave them.'

Kenzie paused. She watched the baby rabbit flail, every movement edging it closer to the verge of the pond. Still, it screamed.

'I can't, I'm sorry.'

Kenzie stood up and stepped closer to the dueling pair. The rabbit was so tiny, tiny enough to still need its mother.

It was probably snatched from its burrow. Kenzie could feel its thick fear, see the wild craze in its eyes.

She was inches away now, but they were so close to the pond, with its tightly woven briars and opaque water. If the rabbit fell through the cracks of those, it would surely drown.

Kenzie waved her arms and the stoat bolted away. For a split second, the rabbit held still but then, seeing Kenzie so close, ran towards the pond.

'No,' Kenzie breathed, leaping after it. The rabbit caught itself on the thorns; Kenzie could see one embedded in its neck. She reached out and clasped the tiny body. It was feverish, heart beating too fast. It tensed in her hands. Kenzie expected it to scream again as she pulled it free of the thorns, but the rabbit only sagged, too fearful now to fight.

Earlie stepped up to her side.

'It's bleeding,' Kenzie said, showing her the side of its neck which was soaked in red.

'It will die,' Earlie said, reaching out a finger to stroke it. 'It was meant to die.'

'Not very vegan of you.' Kenzie pulled the rabbit against her. 'There's a little sanctuary,' she said. 'Kinda near mine. It takes in birds and things like that. I'll give them a ring and see if they can do anything. Here, can you hold it.'

Kenzie put the rabbit into Earlie's arms who brought it close and cradled it against her. The rabbit, still vibrating with the speed of its own heart, laid still. Earlie bent her head and ran her lips over the rabbit's fur, much as Kenzie had done her shoulder.

Kenzie pulled out her phone and looked up the number. As she spoke with a volunteer over the phone, she watched the rabbit slowly calm.

After ringing off, Kenzie tucked her phone away. 'Still alive,' she said, motioning towards the rabbit.

Earlie smiled, running a thumb over the rabbit's back. She stepped close to Kenzie and looked over the planes of her face intently.

'Such compassion,' she said.

Kenzie looked away, shuddering. 'Those screams were horrible. The sanctuary said we can go drop him off. Let's get there quickly.'

∾ ∿

The sanctuary was only small, consisting of a garden shed which had been converted to hold all manner of tanks and cages. As Kenzie watched the volunteer check over the rabbit, Earlie wandered up and down the aisle, peering into the cages full of rabbits and birds and mice.

'He'll be just fine, I reckon,' the volunteer said. She held the rabbit down on the table, parting his fur with firm, careful fingers. 'He's just in a bit of shock at the moment. He'll be alright once he comes down.' The woman glanced behind her, to where a cage sat. 'He's kind of lucky actually. We just had another rabbit come to us yesterday, about the same age. I'll keep the two of them together until they're old enough to be released. Where did you find him again?'

'On Salkings Hill.'

The woman nodded. 'I'll release them back into the same area.'

'Sweet, thank you. Glad he's okay.'

Kenzie looked around for Earlie. She was at the back of the shed, peering intently into one of the tanks.

'Earlie?'

Earlie looked over her shoulder.

'All's good. We can go now.'

With one last look into the tank, Earlie turned away.

Back on the street, Kenzie let out a breath. 'So that was bloody intense.' She took hold of Earlie's hand. 'Some date, eh?'

'The best I've ever been on,' Earlie replied.

Kenzie laughed. 'You're such a weirdo.' She brought Earlie's hand to her mouth and kissed it. 'But I love it.'

Earlie chuckled. She seemed distracted and kept glancing down at her left.

'What is it?' Kenzie asked.

Earlie brought her hand up, unfurling her fingers as she did. From her palm sprang a tiny pied wagtail.

'The fuck Earlie?' Kenzie breathed. 'Did you steal a bird?'

The bird lingered, hovering around Earlie's head. When Kenzie lifted a hand towards it, it flew away, only to return a second later once she'd lowered it.

'He didn't like being in a cage,' Earlie said. 'He told me so.'

'Did he?' Kenzie asked absently, in awe at what she was witnessing. 'How are you even doing that?'

Earlie glanced up at the bird flying in fitful arcs around her. 'He's only thankful. In a moment, he will go.'

As predicted, the bird only stayed with them for a few more minutes. Then it tucked its wings and dove through some shrubbery into a field beyond.

Kenzie watched it go, then turned back to Earlie who was looking at her with a small, pleased smile.

'God, I've never been so attracted to you,' she said, kissing her hard on the cheek. 'That was mint.'

CHAPTER 19

Kenzie plonked herself down on Asa's unmade bed, flicking a pair of boxers onto the floor with a curled lip. The smell of burned pizza drifted in from the kitchen below, vying with the smell of curry spices from one of the houses up the road. The window was open; Kenzie could hear kids out on the pavement below having a water fight.

'Here you are.' Asa returned with two plates and as many cans of beer.

'Thanks, mate.' Kenzie took the proffered cutter and began slicing. The cheese, blackened around the crusts, flaked off and dotted the blue duvet beneath her.

'You're gonna be fucked at uni,' she said. 'Can't even cook a pizza.'

'Piss off. It's Mum's oven. It's naff.'

Asa took a seat on his computer chair which rocked back precariously with his weight. They ate in silence for a few moments before Asa, with his mouth full, asked, 'So, where's Earlie tonight?'

Kenzie shrugged. 'Dunno. Don't really know where she stays.' Kenzie snorted softly. 'Literally don't know anything about her. She's so secretive. Drives me mad but I also kind of love it.'

'Masochist,' Asa muttered. He blobbed a big mound of ketchup onto his plate before passing the bottle to Kenzie. 'So, you reckon it's serious then?'

'Dunno,' Kenzie said again, quietly. 'Like I know I'm off

to uni soon and she's just on holiday but…'

'But you've got the feels.'

'Yeah,' Kenzie sighed. 'Yeah, I fucking do.'

'Well, there's these things called trains.'

Kenzie rolled her eyes. 'Good one.' She fell quiet for a few moments, trying to figure out what she was feeling, and what it was she wanted—things she hadn't allowed herself to think on before. She hadn't realised how much the whole thing was affecting her. She'd tried her damnedest to play it cool, to go with the flow, but now she was here, trying to unravel it all, she found it clogged up inside her like a lump of something indigestible. It was a heavy, frantic sensation, centered squarely around her heart.

'It's like…I dunno. I know we've only been on a couple of dates and I barely know her but I just *know* I'll never meet anyone like her again. Not ever. She's just…she's just amazing.' Kenzie shrugged. 'Just the way she is, the way she doesn't give a fuck about what people think about her, the way she looks at the world differently to anyone I've ever known and all these little things. I just feel so good when I'm with her. She has this energy which is just so different to any other girl I've been with. She just makes me feel free.'

Asa nodded slowly, his pizza all but forgotten as he listened to her intently. He was probably jealous, Kenzie thought wryly. Asa, her best friend, eternally obsessed with love.

'She is fucking gorgeous,' he finally said.

'Alright,' Kenzie murmured, smiling. 'Didn't think she was your type.'

Asa waved her away. 'Not in a het way, more in a *I-want-to-put-her-in-a-glass-cabinet-and-look-at-her-for-enternity* way.'

Kenzie burst out laughing. 'That's fucking dark, man.'

Asa grinned. 'So I take it you've shagged her then?'

Kenzie rolled her eyes. 'So crude. Yes, I've slept with her.'

Asa raised his eyebrows. 'Any good? Better than the last one?'

'Super good.' Kenzie shook her head slightly. 'Like, she's super, super wild. And this is *waaay* TMI but she doesn't shave—you know, down there—and her pubes are the same colour as her hair. Like almost pure white.' Kenzie grinned around a rind of pizza crust. 'I can't work out if she dyes it down there or what.'

Asa laughed, shaking his head. 'You kinky bitch.' He saluted her with his beer can. 'Glad to see my best bud getting some, anyway. Been a while.'

'Too damn long,' Kenzie agreed.

'You can make it work, you know,' Asa said, all teasing gone from his voice. 'If you really wanted to. Sometimes I think, that with Aaron—'

'Aaron was a dick.'

'Yeah, I know but…I just think if you really, really want something, you can't just be all wishy-washy and let it pass you by. Life's too short and all that.'

Kenzie nodded, pursing her lips. Inside, that frantic feeling increased. 'Wise words, my dude.'

Asa threw down a crust, breaking the serious mood. 'You should bring her out one night,' he suggested. 'Here, to Leeds. So I can meet her properly, now that you're a thing.'

'Yeah, I'd like that actually.' Kenzie nodded her head. 'Let's do it.'

CHAPTER 20

Earlie walked slowly down the central avenue of the apple orchard, the hem of her dress dragging over the tiny white flowers dotting the ground. Her face was turned up, eyes running over the boughs of huge, red apples. Always ripe for picking here, always sweet and crisp and juicy.

Still, she frowned. They just weren't right, not these ones, so she continued on.

The orchard became wilder, the apple tree branches thickening and tangling with briars which were so prevalent in the unseelie court. Here, the birds didn't sing. The sound of voices from the lakeside fell away. Earlie brushed through the foliage, her silvered cheeks leaving residue on the leaves. A twig snapped somewhere behind her, making her eyes flicker like an animals'.

She'd been aware of the person behind her for a while. They weren't very clever, stomping on all the fallen leaves and twigs with their long-heeled shoes. When Earlie stopped, her pursuer did too. Closing her eyes, Earlie leant forward and breathed in the apples on her left.

Finally, the person trailing her let herself be known with an aggrieved tut.

Without turning, Earlie said, 'Go away, Risarial.'

'An apple for your lover?' Risarial emerged from the trees, her beautiful face marred with a frown.

'A favour which needs returning,' Earlie replied, releasing the apple branches.

Slithering up the trunk of the tree next to her was a black snake. When Risarial turned her gaze on it, it wound itself into a defensive coil.

'I don't believe you truly love her,' she said, glancing away from the snake. 'You've never loved a thing in your life.'

Earlie felt a spike of anger. She furled her fists, arms stiff at her sides.

'I am very attached.'

Risarial looked her up and down. 'You are still wearing glamour.'

'I am playing,' Earlie snapped.

'Oh, is that it?'

'Yes. Quite.' Earlie craned her head, pirouetting slowly on the spot. 'Now, if you have to be here, why don't you pluck that apple for me right there.' She shot Risarial a withering glance. 'I find I cannot quite reach it with this body.'

Risarial reached up, effortlessly pulling the apple from its branch. She held it out, then when Earlie moved to take it, snatched it back. 'You know you can't stay? You can't, Earlie.'

Earlie said nothing, only seized the apple. It was large; she needed her two human hands to hold it. Like all the mortal fairy tales of old, it gleamed red and glassy. Earlie smiled. Yes, this was the one.

CHAPTER 21

On the first day of August, Kenzie woke up with a knot in her stomach. She rolled onto her back and regarded her ceiling pensively, trying to figure out why she was feeling what she was feeling.

The gnawing had begun the day before, on her walk with Jenkins. They'd gone to the park and Kenzie had noticed how leaf-ladened the verges were. Brown leaves. Autumn leaves. It seemed like summers were ending earlier and earlier these days. She'd said the same thing last year but it hadn't held the same significance as it did now.

There was a knock on her door, then her mum was filling up the doorway, cup of tea in hand.

'Just bringing you a cuppa,' she said, swapping the mug with two glasses on Kenzie's bedside table. 'Take your cups down, madam. How many times do I have to tell you?'

'Sorry,' Kenzie muttered.

Her mum wandered over to her window and pulled open the curtains.

'Heard anything about your accommodation yet?' she asked, taking a quick glance outside.

'No.'

'Taking their sweet time, aren't they? Maybe you ought to get onto them.'

'Maybe.' Kenzie pulled herself up, settling back against the headboard.

'What's up with you mardy-pants?' her mum asked,

gently backhanding the top of her arm.

'Nothing,' Kenzie replied. 'Just tired.'

'Alright. Well don't forget we go away the day after tomorrow. I was thinking we might go up mid-morning, get there for lunch. Maybe go to a pub or something. Somewhere the dogs can go.' Her mum walked over to her laundry basket and picked it up. 'I'll wash all this so it's clean on time.'

With that, her mum left the room.

A panicky feeling clawed at Kenzie. She'd forgotten all about the trip. They visited Auntie Lynne—her mum's sister—every summer. She had a pack of Bernese Mountain Dogs which Jenkins adored, and a hot tub in the back garden. Auntie Lynne had wanted one last blowout with her before she buggered off to uni. A week-long blowout. A week without seeing Earlie. Who knew if she'd still be here by the time she got back.

Kenzie hit her head back against the headboard. 'Shit.'

❧ ⬝

'Your energy is as dull as an unpolished blade.'

Kenzie snorted softly. 'Sounds about right.'

They sat by the stream this time, with Jenkins sniffing along its shallow bank, tail high. The dog still didn't like Earlie, growling at her every time she came near. Kenzie wouldn't admit it aloud, but it kind of perturbed her. Jenkins was the type of dog who loved everyone.

Earlie lay over Kenzie's lap, hands tucked under her face like a sleeping child. Kenzie was stroking her hair but she was barely feeling the strands between her fingers. For once, her mind was faraway.

Earlie rolled onto her back and looked up at her with narrowed eyes. 'What is the matter?'

Kenzie drew in a breath then let it out noisily. 'Basically, I have to go and visit my mum's sister in a couple of days, for a week, maybe longer. I really don't want to go.' She reached out and took Earlie's hand. 'I just want to see you.'

'Don't go.'

Kenzie flew out her other hand. 'I've got no choice.'

'The leaves are beginning to brown,' Earlie said quietly. 'Soon, I will be gone.'

Kenzie sighed. 'I'm sorry, I know it sucks.'

'The night falls faster,' Earlie went on, 'and the birds ready themselves for flight.'

'Earlie, stop. No point making me feel bad about it.'

Earlie's nostril flared, her chest rising and falling quickly. She sprang to her knees and came to Kenzie's front.

'You *cannot* go.'

'Earlie.' Kenzie murmured, a touch bewildered. 'I have to.'

'*No.*'

Earlie closed her eyes and released a breath. When she opened them again, Kenzie flinched at how dark they were. Putting her mouth to her ear, Earlie parted her lips and began to whisper.

⤳ ⤝

Kenzie stood in the dim of the kitchen, watching her mum gardening from the open doorway. She was leaning over a clump of weeds, trowel in hand. On her fingers were the patterned gardening gloves Kenzie had got her a few Christmases back.

For some nonsensical reason, the sight angered her.

A kernel had been blooming in her gut since her meeting with Earlie. Now she was here, back home, with her mum in her eyeline, she all but tingled with the need to say her bit. It was rare she ever spoke out against her mum; they generally had a very agreeable relationship but she resented that now. She resented it with her whole heart.

Blowing out a breath, Kenzie entered the garden.

'Mum?'

'Yep?'

'I'm not going to Auntie Lynne's.' Her hands curled at her sides.

'What?' Her mum looked up, squinting in the sun. ''Course you are.'

Kenzie shook her head. 'No, I'm not. I'm not going.'

'Kenzie, love, you are. We've had this planned for months now.'

'I'm not going. Just listen to me.'

Kenzie's mum paused, straightening up. 'Why do you not want to?'

'Because—there's only a few weeks until I go to uni and a few weeks until Earlie's holiday ends and she goes home and I want to spend as much time with her as I can.' Now she'd said it, she hoped the frantic beating of her heart would calm, but it only sped up.

'Earlie?' Her mum scoffed lightly. 'You've known Auntie Lynne all your life, think she comes before some girl you've just met.'

The anger in Kenzie's gut churned. 'Fuck you, Mum. I'm not going, alright. Why don't you just fucking listen for once?'

'Kenzie!' Her mum's eyes widened, trowel limp in her hand.

'You should probably shut your mouth before someone punches it.'

'What the hell has gotten into you?' Her mum's voice rose.

'You, for fuck's sake!' Kenzie threw up her arms and took a step backwards. Her heart thumped hard, a headache rising to match. The churning turned to a roil. She was out of control, and she couldn't stop and she hated it and *fuck* it felt so good. The words began tumbling out of her. 'Why would I want to go on holiday with you and Auntie Lynne, anyway? You're both pathetic. Both single and lonely. *Desperate.* Do you know how gross it is to go to the pub with the two of you and watch you leer at guys all night? Married guys, guys who wouldn't look twice at you. It's fucking gross!'

'*Kenzie,*' her mum whispered.

'What? It is gross.' Kenzie laughed slightly. 'You're so damn embarrassing. I hate going out with you sometimes, you know. You never dress nice, your hair is always so bloody messy. Try and brush it sometime! You're only forty but you look more like sixty in those baggy dresses you always wear.' Kenzie ran her eyes over the mud-smeared dress her mum wore now, lip curled in a sneer.

Her mum was shaking her head. Her cheeks were red with anger and there were tears in her eyes.

'Oh yeah, go and blub.' Kenzie rolled her eyes. 'You're good at that. Do you know what an ugly crier you are? Your face puffs out like a baboon's fucking asshole.'

'Stop it!' her mum shrieked. She pulled off her gloves with shaking hands. 'Just stop it.'

She turned away from Kenzie and let out a strangled sob. She tried to say something but couldn't for the tears.

'I don't know what's gotten into you.' Her voice hitched. 'I don't know if it's because of this girl, or what, but you better sort it out, alright?' She stood still for moment, trying to collect herself then, with a harsh sigh, pushed past Kenzie. 'Bloody stay here then, I don't want you going after what you've just said.'

The back door slammed.

The anger ebbed; the roiling calmed. For a moment, there was only stillness before the guilt slammed into her. It hit with such a force, she almost doubled over.

'*Fuck.*' She raised shaking hands to her eyes. Tears flooded her vision, and she bit her lip until she tasted blood.

She could hear her mum now, sobbing loudly in her room through the open window. Kenzie squeezed her fists until they hurt. She turned to go inside. She couldn't stand to listen to that any longer.

CHAPTER 22

When Kenzie left her bed the next day, the house was empty. It was a loud emptiness, pressing and heavy. Her mum was gone, and so was Jenkins. When Kenzie went to scrounge up some cereal, she found a note on the dining table.

Gone up to Lynne's early with the dog. You got your wish. Don't trash the place, and you better be in a better mood when I get back. An apology wouldn't go amiss either. Mum x

Kenzie sighed, feeling those bastard tears come into her eyes again. She felt like absolute fucking shit about what she did yesterday. All those things she flung at her mum. She didn't even know where any of it had come from, it just fell from her lips like some gushing black tide. She'd made her mind up to apologise first thing but now she couldn't even do that.

Kenzie ate her cereal, suddenly in the mood to get very, very drunk.

After she left a note for Earlie, she wasn't sure what to do with herself. She unearthed her diary and hastily jotted down her shit-show of a day. She hadn't been in the mood to open her curtains so she sat straining her eyes in the dimness.

After that, she went down to the corner shop and bought herself a cheap bottle of vodka. She debated on opening it then and there but thought better of it. She hated dwelling on things and feeling all angsty and the alcohol, she knew, wouldn't help that. She'd save it for later when she met with Earlie. She only hoped she'd receive her message in time. For the first time, she felt annoyed at Earlie's lack of phone.

For the next few hours, she watched telly and messaged back and forth with Asa. He'd gone out the night before and was convinced he'd met the love of his life. Kenzie gave it a week, tops, before the cards of that particular endeavor came tumbling down.

By 4pm, she couldn't wait any longer. She whistled for Jenkins, then shook her head when she remembered he was gone. She still hadn't apologized to her mum, either. The guilt twisted like a knife.

Instead of a message waiting by the tree, Earlie stood there, clothed in a gauzy wraparound dress.

'Hey,' Kenzie said, smiling wanly.

Pushing off the tree, Earlie smiled back. It was playful and adoring and began to chip away at the heavy mood which had settled around her since yesterday.

Reveling in the lightness she suddenly felt, Kenzie pushed Earlie back against the tree, kissing her soundly. 'You're a sight for sore eyes,' she murmured. Stepping back, she hefted the bag on her shoulder. 'Got us some voddy for tonight.'

'I have something for you too.'

'Oh yeah? What?'

Earlie kissed her lightly on the lips. 'Later,' she whispered.

Kenzie took her hand and gave it a squeeze. 'Can't wait. Come on. Bit of a walk to the place I put in my message. Hope that's okay.'

As they walked, Kenzie glanced down at Earlie and smiled wryly. 'Why do you never have any stuff on you?'

'I have all I need,' she replied.

'But I thought you had something for me?' Kenzie grinned. 'Is it you? Is that what you meant?'

Earlie's face was inscrutable. 'You will see soon.'

Just past the farmers' fields was a long-abandoned quarry, nestled in a small forest of silver birch trees. It was there Kenzie and her friends would hang out sometimes, drinking and warming themselves on rashly erected campfires.

It was there, actually, where Kenzie had her first kiss with a girl. The place was often deserted but the ghosts of visitors were always visible in the way of crushed beer cans and banked fire pits.

'Hopefully we have the place to ourselves,' Kenzie said when they reached it. She pulled off her tent bag and dumped it on the grass near to an ashy pit and a couple of logs.

'We will, do not fear,' Earlie replied.

'I like your confidence.' Kenzie squatted down and unzipped the bag. 'Just gonna set this up quick.'

As Kenzie fiddled with the tent, Earlie entered into the nearby trees, walking between them slowly and touching her hands to the smooth trunks as she passed. It took Kenzie double the time it usually did to set up the tent, her attention split between that and the girl who walked so enchantingly among the trees.

'All done,' she called, straightening the last support. The tent was getting more lopsided with every use, but Kenzie reckoned it would hold for another night.

When Earlie returned, Kenzie nodded towards the tent. 'Want to test it out?' She stepped forwards and put her hands to Earlie's hips. 'I've missed touching you.' She spread her hands, running them slowly over Earlie's bum.

Earlie smiled against her mouth and bit her lip. 'I would rather do it outside of it.'

'Little exposed here,' Kenzie murmured.

'We are alone, I said so.'

Raising her head, Kenzie looked around. They were alone for now, but she doubted it would stay that way.

'Alright,' she finally said. 'I need some alcohol if we're gonna do this.' She ducked into the tent quickly, returning with vodka in hand. 'Want some?'

Earlie's eyes fell to the bottle. 'What is it?'

'Vodka. Only cheap stuff but will do the job. I have mixer too. One sec.'

This time Kenzie returned with a large bottle of coke which she unscrewed and dumped out a quarter onto the grass. Earlie watched the hissing bubbles sink into the mud. Balancing the bottle between her knees, Kenzie topped it up with the vodka.

'There,' she said, taking a swig. 'Sheesh, that's strong. Here.'

Earlie took the bottle gingerly and brought it to her lips. 'The bubbles are tickling my nose,' she said, wrinkling it. She took a sip, her face impassive as she passed the bottle back. 'Curious,' she murmured.

Kenzie laughed. 'Oh my god, you are so cute.' She darted forwards and planted a kiss on Earlie's cheek. 'You'll like it the more you drink it, promise. This is the shit we grew up on. When we were younger, there were rumours it was dodgy after this girl got absolutely paralytic on it. Weirdly enough, it just made us buy it all the more.'

'I love hearing about your life,' Earlie said softly. 'You are fascinating.'

Kenzie snorted. 'Hardly, but thanks.'

Placing the bottle down beside her, she wiggled backwards until her back brushed up against the tent.

'C'mere,' she said, beckoning Earlie over. Earlie rose and came to straddle Kenzie's lap. 'I reckon we'll be safe,' she said quietly, 'if we do it like this.'

Kenzie let her hands drift up Earlie's thighs and under her dress. Earlie nodded wordlessly and tipped her head back, the ends of her hair touching the grass beneath her.

Kenzie's breath caught. 'You're not wearing any

knickers.'

Earlie chuckled breathlessly. 'It seems I am not.'

Kenzie shook her head. 'Wild thing.'

She pressed her lips to Earlie's chest and maneuvered her hands up further.

CHAPTER 23

That night, they dined on pasties and a packet of biscuits. In the shop, Kenzie had checked carefully that they were both suitable for vegans, but Earlie was still picky when eating them. It made Kenzie wonder what kind of food she was into but whenever she made to ask, her thoughts became clogged and she couldn't quite articulate the question. She wasn't sure why as she wasn't exactly the shy type but then again, she felt all kinds of new things when it came to Earlie.

By the time the sun had set behind the trees, Kenzie was pretty buzzed on the vodka. Earlie had refused any further imbibement. Kenzie probably should have stopped too but she was still on a mission to dispel her earlier mood.

Having Earlie there definitely helped, feeling that thrill all over again at just how easily her body responded to her touch. She couldn't be sure she'd ever find that in anyone else again and frankly, that thought depressed her. Kenzie washed it down with more vodka.

'So,' she began, 'what is this thing you have for me?'

They sat on logs now, around a fire which Kenzie had raised using firelighters she'd had the foresight to buy from the shop. She wasn't sure she liked having Earlie sat so far away but the flames licking up into the air and throwing shadows over her face were most becoming. When Earlie smiled, the shadows deepening and darkening, Kenzie didn't think she could ever look away.

Earlie got up and rounded the fire. She sat beside Kenzie, one arm behind her back. When she brought it around to her front, resting in the palm of her hand was the biggest apple Kenzie had ever seen.

'Woah, where the hell'd you pull that from?'

Earlie said nothing, only pushed the apple into Kenzie's hands.

'For you,' she said.

'Is it real?' Kenzie brought it up to her nose. 'God, that smells amazing.'

'As it will taste.'

Kenzie's mouth began to water. She swallowed, wiping her lips with her other hand. 'Can I eat it? Now?'

'I insist.'

Kenzie licked the red, glossy skin then took a bite. Juices filled her mouth immediately, spilling over her lips. 'God,' she murmured, holding the dripping apple away from her as she chewed. 'That's good.'

Earlie watched, chin resting on the palm of her hand.

Kenzie took another, bigger bite. The apple yielded like a peach. It tasted almost fermented; far too sweet, a hint of fizz.

'Why is this so good?'

Earlie smiled, reaching out to run a fingertip down Kenzie's arm. 'I'm so happy you like it. It shows your truth.'

'What do you mean?'

'Only that if it hadn't, the juices would turn black, turning to tar in your stomach.' Earlie leaned forward, resting her forehead against the top of Kenzie's arm. 'That would have made me so very sad.'

Kenzie's teeth brushed the core of the apple. She ate it, seeds and all. Throwing the stem into the fire, she sagged on the log. Her stomach was full, sated; she knew she'd never be hungry again.

Suddenly, her vision wavered.

'Earlie,' she breathed, putting a hand up to her head. It lurched, dizzyingly. 'Everything's tilted.'

Earlie came to kneel at her front, hands on her cheeks. 'Everything's *real*. Look.'

Earlie moved away. Kenzie blinked sluggishly, head tipping backwards to look at the tops of the trees. Their trunks glowed white, their branches high enough to pierce the moon. Tiny lights—fireflies, fairies—drifted through the forest, alighting on flowers which bloomed as they passed.

Kenzie stumbled to her feet. Her eyes found Earlie. She was taller too, her face too bony, too beautiful.

She said, 'I wanted to be bare with you. Truly bare, as you have with me. Come, dear human. Can you hear the music?'

Kenzie could then. Flutes and fiddles and pipes, sounding from somewhere she couldn't see. Earlie reached out and pulled her closer to the fire. 'Dance,' she whispered.

Earlie twirled and her gauzy dress turned to glitter. Kenzie watched her naked body as it turned in the dusty mud. She wanted to dance like that too but she could only tap her feet in some frenzied rhythm, upsetting the ash in the firepit.

Behind a tree, a badger poked out his head. A fox scurried past him, issuing a scream that startled an owl on the branch above. In the air were a thousand moths. They danced around Earlie, capturing her glitter on their wings and bestowing more. Still, Kenzie danced.

When it felt like her heart might stop, Kenzie dropped to the ground and rolled onto her back. The music fell away but still Earlie wore a stranger's face. She came to straddle Kenzie's hips. Her clothes, like Earlie's, turned to powder.

Kenzie's skin burnt as hot as the fire at her feet. Where Earlie touched her, she was sure she blistered.

'More,' she said. 'More.'

She heard twittering then and opened her eyes. Behind Earlie, behind the trees, were faces. Cruel faces. Jeering faces. They were green and twisted and hideous.

'Ignore them,' Earlie said, her eyes too big, too purple.

'Ignore them.'

Kenzie obeyed.

When she reached the pinnacle, always so quick with Earlie, she gripped on tight, the words, 'I love you, *fuck,* I love you,' spilling from her lips.

Slowly, the fire died until only embers were left, twinkling in the ash like the stars in the sky above.

Earlie began humming, brushing Kenzie's hair back from her forehead, over and over. When her eyes slipped shut, Earlie turned back to the faces behind the trees. They were closer now, huddled together. They had phones in their hands and were taking pictures. Earlie shielded Kenzie from their flashes.

'Get away!' Earlie cried.

She stood and the intruders, seeing something unnatural in her eyes, fled.

Kenzie awoke in the tent just as dawn broke. She was alone and the disappointment of that nearly made her cry. She patted around for a note. Please, let there be a note. Her heart jumped when her hand caught on a slip of paper.

She sat up, using her phone light to read.

I had to leave, my love. Thank you for the dearest of nights. I will treasure it always. Earlie.

Leave? Leave fucking where?

Kenzie flopped back down and groaned.

'Shit.'

She cradled her suddenly throbbing head. The empty coke bottle lay next to her and the mere sight of it made her stomach roil.

She lay there for a few more minutes, but it was no use. The night before was a complete and utter blackout.

Coming up to her knees, Kenzie navigated to standing.

She did so slowly, gathering her belongings and shoving them into her bag before stumbling outside. She looked over the tent and blew out a raspberry. Fuck it. The thing was falling apart anyway.

It was a long walk back home. The bag on her back felt like it was full of bricks. It was barely past 7 when she finally made it back to town. Shops were still closed, the only people on the cobbles being dog walkers and delivery folk. Kenzie stopped once to throw up into a bush. A woman walking a terrier saw her and tutted. Kenzie watched her go blearily, wiping at her watery eyes.

By the time she made it home, her heart was palpitating in a worrying way. She dumped her bag and went straight to the kitchen to pour herself a glass of water. Her mum's note was still on the table. Kenzie made a promise that, after a nap, she would finally apologise.

CHAPTER 24

Hey mum, I'm really sorry about the other day. I really am. Would ring you but don't want to interrupt your holiday. Literally don't know what came over me. I didn't mean any of it, I promise. They were really shitty things to say. Sorry again. If you can forgive me, maybe give me a ring and let me know how things are going with Auntie Lynne and the crew :) x

Kenzie read over the text a few times before pressing 'send' and tossing the phone down on the kitchen counter. It didn't seem enough really, but she didn't think there were words to explain what had come over her the day of their argument.

As she made coffee, her thoughts strayed back to Earlie, her body warming at the memory of them having sex against the tent. She fought the compulsion to go to the tree and leave another note, just so she knew when she'd be seeing her again. She thought that after a nap and some food, her memories might start filling in but they hadn't. She still knew nothing from the moment the sun had set.

Her phone pinged. Thinking it was her mum replying, she put down the cafetière and snatched it up. Then frowned. It wasn't from her mum, it was from Sierra.

Heeeey, it read, *can we meet? xxx*

Kenzie tapped her phone a few times, worrying her bottom lip, before replying, *Yeah, sure. Everything alright?*

Kinda, came the reply, a few minutes later. *I'll explain when*

I see you. Can you do today? Could just come to yours xxx

Kenzie gave Sierra a time. Then she looked around the kitchen, thinking the house could probably do with a once over before she got here.

Kenzie was fluffing the sofa cushions when the doorbell rang. She walked to the hall and opened the door.

'Hey,' Sierra greeted, drawing the word out in the same tone she'd used when ending their relationship years ago. That, and the fact that she was playing with her nose ring, a nervous tic, had Kenzie's hackles up. She turned and led Sierra to the lounge.

'So, what's up?'

Kenzie took a corner of the sofa. Sierra took the other, pulling her legs up and wiggling until she was comfy. She was dressed in a plain hoodie and jeans, a combo she'd favoured ever since they were young. Kenzie had never once seen her wearing makeup either. Not that she needed it; Sierra had always been particularly clear-faced and pretty. Kenzie felt a welling of affection for her. She was glad they'd remained friends.

'You want a drink or anything?' she asked, tapping her on the arm.

Sierra waved her away. 'No. I just wanted to show you something before someone else did. Surprised no one's been a dick yet to be honest.'

Kenzie frowned. 'What do you mean? Showed me what?'

Sidling closer, Sierra angled the screen of her phone so Kenzie could see.

'This is being spread around. That guy, Fabian I think. He took it. You know, the one going out with Claire. He was by the quarry last night. Some other people were there too. Henry, Jake and that.'

Sierra pressed play on her phone. A video, blurry at first, then sharpening, showed Kenzie on the ground, naked with Earlie on top of her.

'Oh, fucking hell.' Kenzie covered her eyes with a hand.

'Yeah, kinda bad,' Sierra said. She pulled her arm back, watching the video play on a loop.

'Dude, fucking delete it!'

'I am! I was going to obviously. Just wanted to show you first.'

'Kinda wish you hadn't.'

'Well, better me than someone else.' Sierra tucked her phone away. 'Who is she anyway? Someone from college?'

Kenzie sighed. 'No. No, she's on holiday here. We met last month.'

'*Ooh,* a tourist. Cool.'

'Yeah.' Kenzie shook her head. 'I was so fucking wasted that night. I don't remember a thing.'

Sierra snorted. 'Well, I'm sure people will get over it. You know what this place is like. Plus, you're off to uni soon, aren't you?'

'Yeah, next month. Thank god.'

'Well, there you go then.' Sierra nudged her. 'So, what about this girl? You guys gonna keep seeing each other or end it or what?'

'Dunno mate,' Kenzie said quietly. 'I just don't know.'

☙ ❧

Kenzie glanced at the clock; it was four minutes past midnight. She turned back to her diary and yawned, eyes glossing over the words she'd just written about the night before. She thought she might remember something if she wrote it down. Apparently not.

Kenzie sighed, closing the book and balancing it on top of the digital clock on the bedside table. The thought of Fabian and whoever else filming her during a time she couldn't remember gave her the heebie-jeebies. She wondered if she would tell Earlie about the video or not.

Kenzie turned off her lamp and slouched down beneath the covers. She needed to get up and brush her teeth and make sure the house was locked but first, she'd just rest her eyes.

A pattering at her window made her open them again. She lay there drowsily, wondering if it was hailing outside. The second time the noise came, Kenzie sat up. Definitely not hail. More like little rocks, lots of them, being pelted at her window.

Kenzie got up and peeled back the curtain. Earlie stood on the curbside below. Spotting Kenzie, she stepped up to the front door out of sight. Kenzie dropped the curtain and thundered down the stairs.

'Hey,' she said hushedly, once the door was open. 'This is a nice surprise.'

'May I enter your home?'

'Yeah, 'course.' Kenzie stepped back and let her in. 'Mum's on holiday. She's taken Jenkins so we're home alone.'

Earlie nodded. She started up the stairs.

'I'll be up in a sec,' Kenzie called after her. She locked the front door then jogged to the back to make sure that was locked too.

When she entered her room, Earlie was sitting on her bed, knees up, reading her diary.

'Hey.' Kenzie pulled the book from her hands. 'That's private.'

'A book of Kenzie's thoughts?'

'Yeah. Secret ones.' She slipped it in the bedside drawer, firmly shutting it.

Earlie smiled. 'Am I truly the most beautiful you've ever seen?'

Kenzie sighed. 'Yeah. What of it? You weren't meant to see that.'

'You knew of the people watching us.' Earlie tilted her head. 'How is that?'

'Oh.' Kenzie lowered herself next to Earlie. 'Yeah, so, sorry about this, but my friend Sierra showed me a video someone had taken. Of us.' Kenzie shook her head. 'Super awkward. I was too hammered to notice them. I take it you

118

didn't either?'

'I was aware of others,' Earlie said carefully. 'Little dirty flies. Buzzing and circling.'

'Yeah, it's kind of gross to film someone having sex. Fucking voyeurs.'

Earlie regarded her. 'They have hurt you.'

Kenzie shrugged. 'I'm kind of annoyed, yeah. Mainly just embarrassed.'

'I will humiliate them back.'

Kenzie laughed. 'Oh yeah? Can I watch? Actually, no. I don't really want to see those guys ever again.'

Earlie nodded. 'It is done.'

'Sweet.' Kenzie laid back and pulled Earlie with her. 'You can't sleep in this dress,' she said. 'Want me to get you a t-shirt?' She lowered a strap on Earlie's shoulder. 'Or, you know, you can wear nothing.'

Earlie leaned up, hair enclosing Kenzie's face like a waterfall. She kissed her open lips and whispered, 'The latter.'

CHAPTER 25

'What are you preparing?' Earlie asked, hovering at Kenzie's shoulder.

They were in the kitchen. The backdoor was open and a few house flies had entered, whizzing fitfully around the small room. Kenzie waved the wooden spoon in her hand whenever they came near. On the countertop in front of her was a ceramic mixing bowl.

'Fairy cakes,' she said. 'I do it sometimes for the kids on the trail. I'm working it this afternoon.'

'Fairy cakes,' Earlie mused. 'How fun.'

'Yeah, Mum's a big baker. I kind of picked it up from her.'

From a cupboard, Kenzie pulled down flour and sugar, placing them beside some weighing scales. Flour puffed from the bag, coating the countertop. Earlie ran a finger through it.

'When is your mother returning?'

'Um, I don't know.' Kenzie dug around in the fridge for eggs and butter. 'End of the week maybe. Who knows.'

Earlie put the floured finger in her mouth. 'Hm.'

'I won't be long with this,' Kenzie murmured. 'Then we can go chill or something.'

Using a recipe from an old tattered book, Kenzie quickly made up the batter and dolled it out into cupcake cases.

'Watch out,' she said, shooing Earlie away from the oven. She placed the tray of fairy cakes on a shelf and closed it again. 'Just need to make up the icing now.'

Kenzie was keenly aware of Earlie watching her as she creamed the butter. Earlie reached out and touched her biceps which were hard from her vigorous stirring. Kenzie swallowed.

'Kinda distracting me there.'

Earlie chuckled, drifting away into the garden.

Kenzie added blue colouring to the icing, watching Earlie from the window. A couple of cabbage butterflies fluttered around her. Earlie held still, letting them alight on her hair before they flew up and over the fence.

Kenzie stepped into the garden. 'Hey, want to try some?'

She let Earlie dip a finger into the bowl and put it in her mouth.

'Mm,' she said. 'Buttery sweet. Buttery blue.'

Kenzie smiled indulgently. 'I'll let you lick the spoon when I'm done.'

After the fairy cakes had cooked and cooled, Kenzie spooned on the frosting, making sure there was enough left in the bowl for Earlie.

'Here,' she said, passing it over. 'Go crazy.'

☙ ❧

'So, do you want to come or stay here?'

They sat in the garden, eating a couple of the fairy cakes. The rest were sitting in a shallow box in the hallway so Kenzie wouldn't forget them.

'I will come,' Earlie said. 'I want to see your fairy trail.'

Kenzie smiled. 'You have seen it. It's where we met.'

'I want to hear your version of fairy.'

'Cool.' Kenzie glanced at her watch. 'We'll have to leave in ten.' She grinned suddenly. 'Wait here a sec, just had an idea.'

Kenzie stood up from the grass and bounded upstairs. In the corner of her bedroom, on top of a plastic storage box, were the fairy wings.

Back in the garden, she held them out to Earlie. 'Will you humour me and wear these? They'll go so well with your dress and hair.'

Earlie stood up cautiously. Kenzie rounded her, helping to slip the straps over her arms.

'Not all fae folk are winged,' Earlie said.

'Well, my fairy girl is.' Kenzie stepped back and regarded her. 'God, you suit that look so much. The kids are gonna love you.'

Earlie smiled. 'As you do.'

Kenzie shrugged. 'Maybe,' she said. 'Hey, stick out your tongue.'

When Earlie did, Kenzie laughed, pointing at her. 'Dude, your tongue is so blue. From all that icing.'

Earlie pressed her fingers to her tongue. 'Oh dear. Am I marked?'

'Maybe for a couple of hours.' Kenzie checked her watch again. 'Come on, we should probably go.'

ȣ ȣ

Kenzie held her box of fairy cakes away from the swarm of children whilst Earlie gifted them one each. They all scoffed them immediately, smearing their worksheets with blue icing. Kenzie tucked the empty box under her arm and gestured the parents along the path.

'So, I picked up this book,' one of the mums said. Keeping an eye on her twin boys running ahead, she flicked through *Harmon Blythe's Under Purple Hill: The Cunning Folk of the North*. 'It says this is the wood where some farmer came across two fairies one night.'

Kenzie nodded. '*Mm-hm*. He danced with them all night, eating their food and stuff. They were twins; one light-haired and considered benevolent, the other dark and pretty much evil. When sunrise came, he had to choose between going with them to Fairy or staying here. The evil one wanted him to go with them.'

'What did he choose?' the woman's husband asked. Grinning at his sons, he said, 'I always knew there was something freaky about twins.'

'He chose to stay,' Kenzie said. 'His wife had just given birth and the good fairy said he had to be with them otherwise the fairies would take them too.'

'They wouldn't have,' came Earlie's quiet reply. She walked at Kenzie's side, slightly off the trail, toeing her way through the roots and leaves on the verge of the path.

'Hm?' Kenzie asked. The rest of the group were looking at her too.

'They would never have taken a family,' she said. 'The court has no use for them. Humans belong here, unless it is decided that they don't. The child may have been taken, fostered to a family as a pet. The mother perhaps for a nursemaid. The man—a plaything.' Earlie shook her head. 'We don't take whole families.'

Kenzie pursed her lips in bemusement, nodding slowly. 'Okay,' she said, not missing the baffled glance the woman threw to her husband.

Following a few more stories, they came to an open space on the trail, dotted with wooden play equipment. The kids gave their worksheets to their parents and ran off to play. Earlie followed them. A little girl took her hand and guided her towards a wobbly wooden bridge.

'She's been great, that one,' a man said, gesturing at Earlie. 'The kids really fell for her. Well, mine did anyway.' He chuckled. 'Not the brightest spark, maybe.'

Kenzie smiled, watching Earlie as she encouraged a couple of the kids over the bridge. When they jumped off the other end, Earlie grinned and lifted them up by the arms before setting them back down. She still wore her wings and woodchips dirtied the hem of her dress.

Kenzie turned away. 'Well folks. This is the end of the trail. If you have any more questions, now's the time to ask them.'

Kenzie spent the next fifteen minutes fielding questions,

mainly about Harmon Blythe's fairy lore. It seemed Earlie's peppered comments had stirred up a renewed interest in the subject. Others asked for restaurant recommendations and places to take their kids. At last, the parents let her go, gathering up their broods and ushering them off the trail. Kenzie looked around for Earlie but was unable to see her.

Starting off in the direction they'd come from, she rounded a corner, spotting Earlie on the forest path, a small curly haired boy in front of her. As she watched, the boy tried to run away but Earlie darted forward and grasped his hand, pulling it above his head. The child shrieked, face screwing up into a frown. Pulling away from Earlie's grip, he ran past Kenzie and back towards the playground.

'Dude.' Kenzie watched him go. 'What'd that kid ever do to you?'

'That child is not human,' Earlie said, looking after the boy. 'Those parents have a changeling.'

Kenzie raised her eyebrows. 'Alright, little fairy. You can break character now.'

Earlie was shaking her head. 'Those parents are not here by accident. That child is trying to get home.'

'Dear me,' Kenzie replied, in a tone her mum would use whenever she played up as a kid. 'Should we inform his parents?'

Earlie shook her head. 'Never. Never ever.'

࿐ ࿐

Kenzie sat up in bed, phone to her ear, eyes on Earlie who lay sprawled beside her, head at the foot of the bed. She lay unblinking, the only movement coming from the gentle rotations of her foot in one of Kenzie's hands. Kenzie thumbed the arch of her foot whilst listening to her mum on the other end of the phone.

'…and then we went to *The Plough*, you know the pub that does Sunday roasts for dogs too?'

Kenzie nodded. '*Mm-hm.*'

'Jenkins had his fill, then scoffed all of poor Elsie's too. Daft thing. She just stood there and let him!'

Kenzie chuckled. 'Sounds about right. She needs to learn to stand up for herself.'

'Yeah, well,' her mum said. 'So, what have you been up to anyway?'

Kenzie squeezed the foot in her hand. 'I've been hanging out with Earlie mostly.'

'You have?' her mum asked. Kenzie winced. Her voice was laced with fake enthusiasm. 'That's nice, love. Still wish you were here though.'

'I know,' Kenzie said quietly. 'I still feel really bad.'

'Well, what's done is done, eh? Just don't ever speak to your mother like that again.'

'I won't, I promise. I—' The phone cut out. Kenzie pulled it away from her ear, giving it a shake. She glanced at Earlie who was sitting up now, gazing at her intently. 'Battery's dead. Weird. It was just on 50%. Hope it's not dying.'

Sighing, she leaned over, fished out the charger and plugged it in.

'Poor Mum,' Kenzie said through a yawn. She stretched back against the headboard, arms above her head. 'Hope she doesn't think I did that on purpose.'

Just as she'd said that, her phone pinged.

'It's come back on.' She picked it back up. 'Got a text from Asa—you know, my mate you met at the campout. Fancy going to Leeds Saturday night? He's just invited us.'

'What is Leeds?' Earlie asked, coming to peer at her phone screen.

'Er, the city? About an hour on the train from here.' Kenzie gave a laugh. 'How can you not know where Leeds is?'

'I'm not from around here.'

'But I thought you were?' Kenzie waved her away. 'Never mind. Anyway, he wants us to go out with him. Do you want to?'

'I will go wherever you ask.'

Kenzie grinned and slapped a palm down on her naked thigh. 'Good answer.'

CHAPTER 26

Earlie sat on the chair in front of Kenzie's mum's dressing table, flitting her eyes over the various cosmetics laid out before her.

'Most of this is really old,' Kenzie said, upending another makeup bag. Lipsticks and mascaras scattered on the table. 'I'm not sure which ones she uses these days.'

She picked up a small eyeshadow palette. 'I'll just do your eyes, I think. Reckon Mum's foundation will be too dark.'

She flicked open the palette. There were four colours; a sparkly white, a sea-foam green, smoky blue and charcoal black. '*Hmm,* the blue I think.' She took a brush and swirled it in the colour. 'I've always loved smoky eyes on girls.'

She moved the brush close to Earlie's face who reared back, eyes crossing as she stared at the tip of it. Kenzie laughed. 'Babe. I'm not going to hurt you. Close your eyes and hold still.'

Earlie did. For a moment, Kenzie marveled at her eyelids, the translucency of them and the fine shimmer that always seemed to be there.

'You are so fucking gorgeous,' she said. Earlie's lips quirked into a smile.

She brushed on the colour and stood back. Earlie remained with her face turned up, lips slightly parted so Kenzie couldn't resist leaning forwards and planting a kiss on them.

'I'll let you do your own mascara,' she said. Earlie blinked open her eyes. 'I'll go find you some kind of jacket. You'll be cold without.'

In her room, Kenzie fumbled through her wardrobe. She had plenty of brushed cotton shirts and denim and leather jackets; all of which would be massive on Earlie, but Kenzie had a thing for girls wearing oversized clothes, especially if they were *her* oversized clothes.

She resurfaced with a mid-blue denim jacket. It wasn't one she wore often; it had jewels on the pocket which she thought were kind of tacky. Not her thing, but she reckoned Earlie would look sexy as hell in it.

When Kenzie returned to her mum's room, jacket in hand, Earlie had put gloss on her lips and stood behind the chair, staring into the mirror. She had on a blue dress tonight, a few shades lighter than the denim jacket. The material was almost sheer, falling to just above her knees and long-sleeved on the arms. It shimmered lightly, just like the lids of her eyes.

'Here.' Kenzie held out the jacket. 'Whack this on.'

Earlie shrugged into it, shaking out the sleeves which hung over her hands.

'C'mere. Let me sort that.' Kenzie began rolling up the sleeves. This close, she caught the scent of something sweet. 'Mm, have you put perfume on?' she asked.

'No.'

'Hm. You smell like honey and flowers.' She stepped back. 'Let me see you.'

Earlie stood still, head high, as Kenzie ran her eyes over her. Her hair was tousled, catching on the jewels of the jacket and her smoky eyes blinked slowly.

'Hot damn,' Kenzie murmured, shaking her head. 'If we didn't have a train to catch, we'd be in my bed in the next ten seconds. Anyway, come on, we best go. We can get some tinnies on the way.'

❧ ❧

The train was busy, having come from a larger city and there was only standing room. Kenzie steered Earlie into a corner and shielded her from a group of rowdy boys. When the train lurched forward, Earlie stumbled, eyes wide as she looked around. Kenzie put her arms around her and kissed her head.

'What beast is this?' Earlie asked.

Kenzie laughed. 'Could be worse. At least we got one of the fancy new electric ones.'

About ten minutes into the journey, Kenzie raised the four-pack of ciders from the floor by her feet and wrangled one free.

'Want a cider?' she asked.

'Apple cider?'

'Yep.' Kenzie passed her one. Earlie inspected her can then, seeing Kenzie pop the lid of hers, did the same.

As more people boarded, the busier and rowdier the train became. The group of boys behind them had unearthed speakers from somewhere and were playing music loudly, much to the disgust of an older couple in the seats beside them.

Earlie smiled, craning her head to the side of Kenzie, trying to catch a glimpse of the boys. In her hand, she scrunched her can in time with the music.

'Can we dance?' she said.

Kenzie turned around to look. The boys looked to be her age, maybe a year or two older, dressed pleasantly and obviously already pissed. Probably harmless, but after the incident on the canal, Kenzie would rather not risk it. 'Um, maybe not. Save yourself for later.'

By the time they pulled into Leeds, Kenzie was glad to escape the hot fug of the train. The station was busy, crammed with people going home after a day of shopping or arriving for a night out or gig. Kenzie took Earlie's hand, pulling her through the throng when she thought she might stop.

'What life!' she said. 'What *stink* as well.'

'Always smells like oil here,' Kenzie agreed.

They ascended some stairs, looped down the other side and exited the station. Still holding Earlie's hand, Kenzie thumbed through her phone.

'Asa's already there.'

'Where?'

'*Quartz*. It's this little gay bar, hole in the wall thing. Kinda shitty but drinks are cheap and it stays open 'til six.'

'Will there be music?'

''Course. And dancing.' Kenzie squeezed Earlie's hand. 'I know how you like to dance.'

They weaved their way through the city centre, steadily veering west until they came to the A-road leading out of the city. The sun was low in the sky already, a far cry from the long, summer days of the previous month. Cars zoomed past with their lights on and as they walked beneath a streetlamp, it flickered to life.

Beside Kenzie, Earlie coughed.

'You alright?'

Earlie nodded, hand to her chest. 'This place is filthy.'

Kenzie took a big breath in. 'It's the city baby.'

Just before they came upon the city's viaduct, they turned down a side street where all the buildings were dark apart from one right at the end. Purple light bled onto the street, highlighting the bald head of a bouncer who laughed with a drag queen. Beyond them, a couple of girls in bodycon dresses smoked cigarettes in the tangled grass at the end of the street.

Under her breath, Kenzie asked, 'Do you have any ID?'

'Any what?'

'Identification. You know, a driver's license or something. Something to show your age.'

'Whatever for?'

Kenzie slowed down, fishing her own out of her pocket. 'To get in. You have to be over eighteen. Have you never been clubbing?'

'Oh,' Earlie said. A smile crept over her face. 'I am sure I am old enough.'

'Well, the bouncer has to be sure too.'

Earlie nodded. 'I will make it so.'

Kenzie regarded her dubiously. They came to the bouncer who smiled and reached out for Kenzie's ID. He barely glanced at it before passing it back. 'Thanks, love.'

Kenzie stepped up to the doorway. She spotted Asa right away and gave him a little wave before turning back to Earlie. She had stepped close to the bouncer and was smiling at him. With a little nod, the bouncer moved aside to let her through.

Kenzie shook her head. 'You shit. He'd never have let me in without ID.' She put her arm around Earlie. 'Helps to be so pretty.'

They met Asa at the bar.

'Getting us some shots,' he said, motioning to the bartender filling three glasses. Kenzie groaned. 'Hey, go hard or go home.' He reached out and kissed Earlie on the cheek. 'Heya, darling. You alright?'

Earlie nodded, her gaze drifting to the LED disco light throwing multicolour circles over the darkened bar. Asa plonked a shot glass in front of her.

'Drink up.'

Without looking away from the shifting, lit-up walls, Earlie plucked her shot glass and tipped it down her throat.

Asa raised his eyebrows, glancing sidelong at Kenzie. 'Not bad, not bad.'

Grinning, Kenzie reached for her own glass and threw it back.

'As sweet as syrup,' Earlie said, gently placing her glass back down.

Kenzie grimaced. 'Yeah, pure sugar that. What would you like to drink? I'll get it.'

'Not something crackly,' Earlie said, peering at all the backlit bottles lining the back of the bar.

'Not something what?' Asa laughed.

'She means fizzy,' Kenzie translated. 'She doesn't like fizzy.' She patted Earlie's back. 'I'll get you a cranberry vodka instead.'

When they had their drinks, they claimed a high-legged table, Kenzie and Earlie sitting on the booth side and Asa on one of the wooden stools.

'So, is this boy meeting us tonight?' Kenzie asked. 'The one you've been texting.'

Asa waved her off. 'No. Fizzled. Got serious fuckboy vibes.'

Kenzie nodded sagely. 'Well, good for you.'

'Yep, so I'm third wheeling tonight, baby.'

'Not if we find you someone,' Kenzie said, raising her pint.

Asa snorted. 'Good luck with that. Not much talent around here.'

'The night is young. Give it time.'

CHAPTER 27

Risarial lay on the bank of the lake, trailing a hand through the lukewarm waters. Every so often, she'd feel an asrai gently nose at her fingers and she'd give it a flick, laughing at the gurgling squeal as it dove back into the depths.

Above her, the perpetually dusky sky was streaked with pink. Another hour, and the stars would be out. More than a few folk were enjoying the evening around them but they knew to keep their distance. Risarial closed her eyes, savouring the peace until a noise at her side rent the air. In the water, her hand closed to a fist.

'Cerulean, the sound of your chamming is driving me to distraction.'

Cerulean grinned, unrepentant as always, and took another bite of her apple. 'Just enjoying the bountiful fruits of this land. I am only sorry Earlie will not be enjoying such things.'

Risarial grunted. 'Earlie needs to come home.'

'Then you will need to catch her by her collar. She seems quite settled.' Cerulean flicked an apple seed into the lake. 'I am quite impatient for my time,' she admitted. 'I feel a peculiar yearning for what lays earthside.'

Risarial opened her eyes. 'Well, no need to wait,' she said. She turned over onto her stomach, face scant inches from the surface of the lake. 'Why don't we see what our youngest sister is up to right this moment.'

Cerulean jumped to her feet and came to the lakeside, following the path of Risarial's finger drawing circles over the surface of the water.

As the water settled, Risarial's pupils dilated, black covering brown. Her eyes were drawn to the shapes taking form in the teal depths. Risarial frowned. There was so much light, so much colour. And noise too, deep and bassy.

Squatting down, Cerulean leaned forward. She could see Earlie now, swathed in smoke—white, icy smoke, blowing from some kind of box in the corner.

'What is that?'

'A club. She's in a club. A place of human revels.' In her eyes was a dark hunger. 'Dank, sticky places.'

'Look at all those humans,' Cerulean hushed. She narrowed her eyes at the blonde boy dancing behind Earlie, sashaying his hips into hers. He was pretty and small but his clothes were ugly and Cerulean could almost smell the dirty human smell of him. 'Look how they move. So very queer.'

Risarial smiled. She ran a finger over the head of one girl, making her ripple. 'So queer.' Craning her head towards Cerulean, she said, 'How would you like to join our dear sister earthside tonight?'

Cerulean raised her face to Risarial. 'There's trouble in those eyes.'

Risarial smiled wider. 'You know how I hate to miss a revel.' She took Cerulean's hands and together they stood. 'You first,' she said.

Cerulean tilted her head, staring out over the lake with sightless eyes. Slowly, her vision cleared and she smiled. As Risarial watched, her sister shifted into a beautiful boy: tight blonde curls, thick, arcing eyebrows and full lips. Her eyes were outlined in black and a silver hoop severed one nostril. She wore stonewashed jeans with a shimmery, khaki-coloured tank top.

'You've been watching them,' Risarial said, looking her up and down, a sly smile on her lips. 'The humans.'

Cerulean shrugged and nodded towards her. 'Now you.'

Risarial drew in a breath. When she released it, eyes closed, her body filled in with curves and her straight hair kinked. Dark colour dusted her eyelids and her lips held the same hue as the apples in the orchard.

It was different to how she usually went. Cerulean raised an eyebrow. 'Lest you're recognized?'

Risarial shrugged her shoulders, running a hand over her rounded stomach. A belly bar winked there. It was in the shape of a star. 'Something like that.'

She sighed, tasting bubblegum, a vestige from the last time she was earthside. Bubblegum and sherbet and aniseed drops. Her mouth watered. She suddenly hungered for earth.

'Come,' she said. 'Let's join our sister at her revel.'

Kenzie pulled Earlie closer, forcing her arms up and around her neck. Two hours later and the dancefloor was packed. A girl in a neon dress attempted to dance around a pole in the middle of the floor and along its edges was a drag queen selling cheesecake shots at two pounds a pop.

Earlie said into Kenzie's ear, 'I have never been to a revel such as this.'

Kenzie smiled and kissed her lips. 'Oh sheltered one.'

They danced for song after song until Kenzie was sweating through her shirt, her cheeks pink and forehead damp. She reveled in Earlie's nearness and how she had eyes for only her. It made her feel kind of…smug. Earlie was simply the most beautiful girl she'd ever set eyes on and judging by the glances from those around them, Kenzie wasn't the only one who felt like that.

A blast of dry ice shot from the DJ booth, smothering the two of them. When it cleared, Earlie looked a little worse for wear. She brushed wild, tangled hair from her face, lips parted and eyes heavy lidded. She fanned her face with a slender hand.

'You alright?' Kenzie asked against the shell of her ear.

Earlie nodded and replied, 'I fear I am too hot.'

'Let's go outside for a bit.' She gestured to Asa but he shook his head, pointing to a couple of his friends who had turned up an hour before. He was no doubt trying to get into the pants of one of them, or at least his phonebook.

Kenzie took Earlie's hand and they escaped outside.

'Wish this place had a smoking area,' she said, leading Earlie to the grass.

Earlie twirled there, her small, moccasin-style shoes tangling in the grasses. 'Oh, what a night,' she sang.

Kenzie smiled. 'You little pisshead.' Looking around, she pursed her lips. 'Wish I had a smoke.'

'Like a pipe?' Earlie reached up and captured a cottonwood seed drifting past. 'My fathers' was blown from the crystal mined from the bottom of Lake Ether. It makes his smoke taste like blueberries.'

Kenzie chuckled. 'I was thinking more of a cigarette, but that sounds good too. You know, I never know if you're making this stuff up or you really live such a whacky life.'

'I never lie,' Earlie said, standing still. 'Never, ever, ever.'

'Whacky life it is then.' She waited a moment before asking, 'How're you feeling?'

'So good.' Earlie twirled again. 'So *alive.*'

Kenzie captured Earlie and held her still. 'You make me feel alive. Do you know that?' Earlie tilted her head. 'I've never known anyone with energy like yours.'

'You said you loved me,' Earlie whispered. 'The night we made love under the silver trees. You said it.'

Kenzie dropped her eyes to the ground. She didn't remember that. She felt a blush in her cheeks and was thankful for the night.

'Yeah, I do,' she said. 'I really fucking do.' She held up her hands. 'You don't have to say it back, don't worry. I know it's mad. You're just on holiday or whatever but'— she shrugged—'that's just how I feel.'

'Kiss me,' Earlie said. 'Kiss me like you did that night.'

Looking around, Kenzie pushed Earlie against the wall of the club. She could feel the bass through the bricks, pulsing through Earlie and into her. Hidden from the streetlamps, they kissed. Kenzie felt the scratchy denim of Earlie's jacket against her heated skin, her narrow fingers clawing gently through the cotton of her shirt.

When Earlie let out a moaning sigh, someone behind them cleared their throat. Kenzie looked over her shoulder, seeing two butch girls standing in the grass, failing to hide their smirks. They each held a cigarette between their fingers. When they saw Kenzie looking, they turned their backs.

Kenzie stilled at Earlie, releasing a shaky breath. 'Best go back.'

CHAPTER 28

They had to push through a queue to reenter the club; the place was swarming now. In the DJ booth, a drag queen was blasting queer classics and there looked to be a hen night going on judging by the number of girls with pink feather boas slung around their necks. Though she tried, Kenzie couldn't see Asa anywhere.

Pulling Earlie towards the quiet end of the bar, Kenzie said, 'Are you drunk yet?'

'I don't know how I'm supposed to feel,' was Earlie's abstracted reply. Her eyes were more glassy than usual, rooted on the arched, red brick behind the bar.

Kenzie stroked her arm. 'Just let me know when you've had enough.'

Sensing Earlie was beginning to wilt, Kenzie ordered them both an energy drink bomb, and a third for Asa.

'Let me know if you see him,' she said, heading to the dancefloor. When she sensed Earlie wasn't following her, she glanced back to where Earlie stood still, eyes fixated on a shadowy spot beneath one of the LED lights.

Following her gaze, Kenzie grinned. 'Looks like he won't be needing this then,' Kenzie said, drinking Asa's drink whilst he writhed with some guy up against the wall. 'We're not gonna hear the end of that later. Shall we go dance and leave them to it?'

Shaking her head viciously, Earlie pushed past Kenzie and headed over, pulling on the other boy's arm. As Kenzie watched, the boy smiled, reaching an arm up to pat Earlie on the head. Kenzie frowned at the look on Earlie's face and made to follow. A hand captured her and pulled her to a stop.

'Want to dance?' a smoky voice said into her ear. Kenzie glanced up into the dark eyes of a girl.

'Actually, that's my girlfriend over there,' Kenzie said, pulling away.

'And that is my friend.' The girl inclined her head towards the boy who still held Asa's wrist.

Kenzie turned to her. 'Oh, you know him?'

'I do.' The girl pouted her lips. 'He left me alone. Will you keep me company?'

Kenzie glanced back at Earlie. She was smiling now, though a frown still showed on her face.

'Come,' the dark-haired girl said, chuckling. 'Let them join us in a while.'

Kenzie wanted to protest but with every step they took towards the dance floor, her arguments fell away. They stepped up onto the raised floor and the girl turned back to her, smiling.

God, she was beautiful. Kenzie was stunned for a moment, letting the girl pull her close. Her body was gorgeous, almost liquid in the way it moved. Kenzie had plenty of curves too but her body felt more masculine, less shapely. There was no way her hips would move like this girls' did. Her stomach was bare, a lacy bralette covering her chest. On her legs was black leather, a diamonte belt threaded around her waist.

'What's your name?' Kenzie asked, her question an excuse to lean closer.

The girls' lips came to her ear. 'Rhiannon.'

'I'm Kenzie.'

Rhiannon smiled. 'I know.'

When the next song ended, Kenzie looked around. Earlie was gone, as was the boy, but Asa was there bearing down on them.

Oh my god, he mouthed, fanning his face. Kenzie grinned. When he reached them, he leaned up and said to Rhiannon, 'Tell your friend he's the best kisser ever!'

Rhiannon smiled slightly.

'Where's Earlie?' Kenzie asked.

Asa shrugged airily. 'Don't care.'

Kenzie whacked him on his arm. 'Dude. Where did she go?'

Rhiannon placed a hand on her. 'I believe they both went outside. Shall we join them?'

Asa nodded yes before she could answer. He pulled on Kenzie's arm. 'We're just gonna get a drink. Meet you outside, yeah?'

Rhiannon gave them a nod and slipped away towards the exit. Kenzie watched her go, rivetted by the sway of her hips.

'Um, eyes,' Asa said, clicking his fingers in front of her face. 'Think of Earlie.'

'Shut up.' She nodded towards the bar. 'I'm good for a drink. I don't want anymore.'

'Tough,' Asa said, pulling her along.

They hid their glasses from the bouncer as they left the club. There were quite a few people on the grass now, smoking and mingling in groups. Kenzie saw Earlie standing amid the trees at the back, mostly hidden from the streetlamps and the purple neon light above the club door. With her was the boy and Rhiannon.

'Oh my god, he's so gorgeous,' Asa said under his breath. 'They all bloody are.'

Kenzie nodded. It was true. When she got to them, she threaded a hand around Earlie's waist.

'So, these are your friends?' she asked, looking between Rhiannon and the boy. She caught him smiling at Rhiannon. It was a strange smile and Kenzie wasn't sure what to make of it. 'From where?'

'We go far back,' Rhiannon said. She had her arms crossed over her chest, peering at Kenzie with an evaluating expression.

Earlie nodded. She put a hand up to her chest, eyes fixed on the ground.

Kenzie gave her waist a squeeze. 'You alright there?'

Earlie nodded again. 'Oh, how my heart beats so.'

'Eek. Probably had a bit too much to drink.'

Earlie raised the hand that had been on her chest. Kenzie could see clearly how it shook.

The boy's gaze sharpened. He shrugged off Asa who'd glued himself to his side. 'Earlie?'

Earlie's mouth parted and she let out a little *oh*.

Kenzie moved to come around to her front, but Rhiannon shoved her to the side.

'Careful,' she said, frowning, holding her drink away from her as it sloshed.

'What has she consumed?' Rhiannon asked, cupping her hands around Earlie's cheeks.

'What? Nothing. Just some drinks.'

Rhiannon whirled on her, face twisted in a snarl. She grabbed Kenzie's chin between pinched fingers and pulled her close. 'Tell me, dirty human, what she has consumed.'

Kenzie wracked her brains, the sudden fear of this girl fogging her mind. 'Um, just some vodka,' she said, 'and a couple of shots, and a cider on the train. And an energy bomb just now. Nothing crazy.'

Rhiannon's eyes sharpened. 'Caffeine?' Kenzie nodded, her brain refusing to make sense of the fact that the girls' eyes were now burning bright orange. She almost fell to her knees when she was released. 'You will be just fine, Earlie.' She brushed tangled hair out of Earlie's eyes. 'But you must come home now.'

She took Earlie by the arm and pulled her deeper into the trees. The boy followed. Asa, seeing him leave, leaped after him. He tripped over something, losing his drink, and the boy laughed.

'Come on little pet,' he said, slapping his thighs. 'Keep going.'

144

'Asa? Wait, what the fuck? Where are you all going?' Kenzie took a few rushed steps forwards but she struggled to see in the dark. 'Earlie? I thought you were coming back to mine?'

'Oh, Kenzie.' Earlie laughed faintly, watching her blunder after them. She still held a hand up to her chest, breathing rapidly. 'Why don't you go home now, sweet one.'

'Or we can take her?' the blonde boy asked. Kenzie squinted her eyes at him. He looked different now, more feminine. 'I heard she favours the apples of our orchard.'

Earlie looked at him sharply. 'No. Not this one.'

'Earlie.' Kenzie shook her head. 'I don't get what's happening.'

'Do not worry your sweet head.' Earlie broke away from the group to blow her a slow kiss. Kenzie stumbled. Something wrapped around her shoes. Thin, muddy vines. They broke from the earth, curling around her ankles.

Kenzie tried to pull herself free but ended up on her knees, clawing at the mud. 'What the fuck?' she breathed. The vines held her tight. Looking up, she watched helplessly as the four of them faded into the night.

CHAPTER 29

The smell of oil roused her. Kenzie stirred, wincing at the pain lancing into her side. Opening her eyes, she saw she was at the train station, slouched over two chairs which dug into her hip painfully. She sat up, eyes drawn to the large clock on the opposite side of the platform. It was 7am.

Kenzie sighed and raised her hands to scrub her eyes. Something whispered against her cheek. Holding her palms up, she saw a piece of blue ribbon tied around her little finger.

Still contemplating the ribbon, she pulled out her phone and checked her messages. None from Asa. She frowned, feeling a surge of anger. She sent a text, asking him where the fuck he was. Wherever it might be, she only hoped Earlie was there too.

When 8am came around, the first train back to Kirkall Bridge pulled up to the station. Kenzie reluctantly boarded. Even when in her seat, she scanned the platform for Earlie, willing for her to appear. When the doors closed and the engines revved up, Kenzie slouched back and sighed.

'Hiya, love.'

Fending off a bouncy Jenkins, Kenzie glanced to where her mum was shoving her holiday washing into the washing machine. It was mid-morning and Kenzie had just got in.

'Hey,' she said. 'Just got back?'

'Yeah, got an early start this morning. I've got some cooking to do for the shop tomorrow. Where have you been?'

'Leeds with Asa.' Kenzie yawned. 'I'm knackered.'

'Have fun?'

'Yeah, until they all bloody ditched me.' Opening the fridge, Kenzie pulled free a carton of orange juice. She wasn't sure how long it'd been in there, but she was so parched she didn't care, and drank straight from the mouth.

Her mum frowned. 'Ditched you?'

Kenzie sighed, fiddling with the cap of the juice. 'Yeah, he met this guy. He was a friend of Earlie's. They all went off…' Kenzie trailed off. That part of the night still made no sense. The ground coming to life, holding her tight so she couldn't follow? And Rhiannon's eyes—what was that about? Did one of her drinks gets spiked somehow? It was something she considered the whole train ride back.

'What and just left you?' her mum continued.

Kenzie shrugged. 'Yeah, basically.'

'What a rubbish thing to do.'

'Ah, well.' Kenzie placed the juice back into the fridge. 'I'm sure I'll get the full story later on.'

Kenzie was dozing on the sofa that afternoon when her phone rang. Blinking her eyes, she saw it was Asa's mum ringing from her social media account. She frowned. Thinking she might be pocket-dialling her, Kenzie waited a few more seconds before putting the phone to her ear.

'Hello?' she said tentatively.

'Hi, this is Carrie.' The voice sounded alert and slightly pinched. 'Is Asa with you, Kenzie?'

'No, I'm at home. Why? Is he not home yet?'

'No, and he's not answering his phone. I was really hoping he was with you. He went out with you last night, didn't he?'

Kenzie sat up. Clearing her throat, she said, 'Yeah, but he went off with someone and kind of left me.'

'What someone?'

'Some guy. Wasn't just them though. There were two other girls too. The boy he met—his friend was with them, and my friend too.'

'Right. And why didn't you go with them?'

Kenzie paused. 'I don't know. I just didn't. This sounds bad, but I was super drunk. I woke up at the train station on my own. I've been trying to reach him too.'

Carrie sighed. 'Alright. Well maybe his phone's just died then. The fact he was with a few people makes me feel better.'

'Yeah,' Kenzie said. 'I'm sure he's fine.'

'I'm sure. Just let me know if you hear from him, alright?'

'Yeah, will do.'

❧ ❧

'Have you seen this?' Kenzie's mum asked later that night. After she'd completed all her cooking for the next market, they both decided on a lazy day on the sofa, the smell of freshly boiled berries wafting in from the jam jars cooling in the kitchen.

Kenzie lifted her head from the arm of the sofa. 'What?'

'This.' Her mum sidled closer, showing Kenzie the screen of her phone. 'Asa's still missing.'

Kenzie looked at the phone. Carrie had made a post about Asa not coming home, detailing his last movements and calling for any information. It all looked very serious, replete with a picture of him and a number to call. Carrie's, she presumed. 'Shit,' she said.

'Think he's alright?'

'Well, yeah. He should be with Earlie. Or that guy.'

'But what if he tried to go home afterwards and something happened?'

'Well, I don't know, do I? I wasn't there but I'm sure he'll turn up. He's probably just with the guy at his. You know how he gets obsessed with boys.'

'*Hmm*. I hope so.'

149

Kenzie sighed. She took out her own phone and typed another text. *Dude?? People are worried. Answer please. She pressed send, adding the message to all the unanswered ones before it.*

CHAPTER 30

'Earlie?' The finger poked her in the side again. 'Earlie?'

Earlie ignored the prodding, giving a little sigh and shake of her head. She kept her eyes fixed on the mist in the middle distance, thinking of her human who waited for her on the other side of it.

Beside her, Cerulean blew out a very undignified raspberry. 'You cannot be angry with us forever.'

'Watch me,' Earlie said. 'You are both nothing but meddlesome, nosy clods.'

They sat in the fluffy grass bordering the vineyards, on a blanket woven with gold and silver threads. On a wooden charcuterie board in front of them were the remnants of noon meal—grape sprigs, olive oil-soaked breadcrumbs and tall-stemmed wine glasses drained to the dregs.

Cerulean sighed again and got to her feet. A few meters away by the trees was Asa, the boy leaping up to capture plums on the higher branches. He had already eaten all within reach.

Somehow, he had lost his clothing shortly after entering the hill, his pale naked body now littered with scratches. The human hadn't stopped gorging himself since arriving. Already Earlie could see the fattening of his face. Judging by the watery glassiness of his eyes, he hadn't slept either.

Cerulean reached over him and pulled down more branches. The boy didn't even pluck the plums, he just bit right into them, juices running in yellow rivulets down his body. Cerulean laughed and reached for more.

He was bound for the bordello once Cerulean stopped playing with him. The lower courtiers did love their human boys. Some of the gentry, too, though Earlie wasn't supposed to know that.

'We have to return him,' Earlie said, a peculiar discomfort filling her at the thought of his fate.

'We do not,' Risarial replied without looking up from her book. It was a thin, tattered collection, stolen from the mortal world. The title read *Queer: An Anthology of Anger*.

'Risarial. It is making Kenzie sad. I can feel her worry and her anger. In here.' Earlie tapped her chest.

'It is high time you gave up this girl.'

'But it was you who struck the bargain!'

Risarial lowered her book. 'Yes. And you have succeeded in making a mortal girl fall in love with you. The bargain is fulfilled.'

'But I'm not sure that I love her,' Earlie confessed quietly. 'And I do abhor the thought of her forgetting me.'

'She *must*.'

Earlie shook her head. 'She does not. Maybe I will make my home there.' She smiled at the mist. 'She can be my mortal forever.'

'Mortals don't live forever.' Sitting up, Risarial's voice turned icy. 'Earlie, that world is not for us. Do you not know how the wild fae there dwell?'

'They are free.'

'No, Earlie. They are not free, you fool. They live in destitution, cooped up in filthy metal fortresses where no human will come looking for them. Choked on iron, *sickened* by it. Their lives shortened. They stagnate just like humans.'

'Stop—'

'And they have no energy to glamour themselves anymore so they must hide, forcing humans to do their bidding so that they are not caught and executed. That is no life for you, Earlie. Nor for your mortal.'

Earlie shook her head. Opalescent tears spilled down her

cheeks. 'You are awful to tell me these things! You are truly, so very awful.'

Risarial grabbed her hand. 'I tell you the truth. Believe it, sister.'

Earlie shook away her touch and stood. 'I am going back. I have things I must complete. Promises to uphold. And you will not stop me.'

Risarial laid back and picked up her book again. 'Maybe not me,' she said. 'But Father, his army. They will come for you. You are an heiress, Earlie. To exile yourself means swift and sure death.'

Earlie drew in a breath. 'That won't be necessary. I will be back before then. But first, I must say goodbye.'

CHAPTER 31

When Kenzie woke up, she checked social media with the same hope in her heart as the previous days. And, just like with them, it was dashed right away. Asa was still missing.

'Fuck.' She released a shaky breath, tossing the phone onto the bed where it bounced once and landed with a thud on the floor. Running a hand through her hair, she closed her eyes.

Despite the fuckedupness of that night, she couldn't help but feel responsible. The whole reason they were out in the first place was so Asa could get to know Earlie. That was her fault. Kenzie began to dread the inevitable daily phone call from Carrie, where they rehashed his last moves over and over again. She always hung up with stabbing guilt and tears in her eyes. At least the police had been notified now. He was being looked for.

Kenzie dragged herself out of bed and ripped off a ribbon of paper from a notebook and penned a quick message. It was becoming a ritual now.

When noon rolled around, Kenzie grabbed the dog and set off for the tree on the fairy trail, jar in pocket. She almost didn't see the new message, so intent on burying her latest jar. Kenzie's breath caught, heart thumping. With shaking fingers, she clawed at the cork, pieces of it breaking off and crumbling in her hand.

'Come on,' she muttered, flicking the bits away.

Finally uncorking it, she upended the note onto the ground and unfurled it.

My love, it read, *please do not think that I have forgotten you. I shall never. I will see you soon but until then, just know you will never have to see those buzzy little dirty flies again. It is done, just like I said. Earlie.*

'The fuck? What the fuck do you mean?' she said aloud, coming to rest against the tree. Jenkins whined and leaned against her. Stroking him absently, she read the note over and over, until it made less sense than the first time she read it.

She shoved the note in her pocket. 'Fuck's sake Earlie.'

છ જી

She took Jenkins into the birch forest, intending to scale the whole stretch of it. She hadn't any lunch on her, but she couldn't bear being at home at the moment. Her mum, forever asking questions and updating her on what Carrie was posting on social media. She was sick of it.

Kenzie felt her phone buzz and took it out immediately, in case it was Asa or an update on the investigation. She knew the police wanted to talk to her soon. It was only a matter of time before they knocked on her door.

Opening the message, she could see it was only from Sierra.

Hey, we got into the old cement factory. Gonna hang out here for a bit. Wanna join? xxx

Who's we? x Kenzie typed back.

Me, Becca, Craig, etc. Basically all of us. We have booze. Pls come xxx

Fabian? x

Yeah, but don't worry about that!! I had him delete everything xxx

Kenzie pursed her lips, thinking. The factory was only on the other side of this stretch of woods, a huge, light-stoned building which had one long chimney reaching into the sky like a church spire. They used to hang out there years back, but the place had since been bricked up and fenced over. Apparently, they'd managed to wiggle their way back in again.

I'm kinda close but I have the dog x, she finally replied.

Bring him!! xxx

Kenzie pocketed her phone. 'Wanna go see Sierra?' she asked Jenkins. He looked up at her, tongue lolling. 'Do ya? Come on then. Good boy.'

The set off east towards factory. Kenzie picked up a branch and threw it for Jenkins who bounded after it through the trees. He returned it a couple of times before losing interest and wandering off with his head down, sniffing. Kenzie followed, catching occasional glances of him stalking between the trees like a great black bear.

She had just seen the first white flashes of the factory through the tree trunks when something up ahead set Jenkins off on a barking spree.

'Jenkins!' Kenzie called. She gave a whistle. 'Shush, will you! Leave those squirrels alone.'

But the dog continued to bark. It was high-pitched and shrill, like the noise he had made when someone tried to break into their cottage a few years back. Kenzie heaved a sigh and jogged after him.

'What have you found—' Kenzie stopped in her tracks.

A few feet in front of them was a hunched over creature, with skin as dark and thick as tree bark, orange eyes and a mouth full of needle-like teeth, thin trails of saliva stretching between them.

'Ah, ah, ah,' it said when it spotted her, flinging out a taloned hand. 'You don't want to go any further.'

'What?' Kenzie asked faintly. She stared at the creature, the utter wrongness of it clouding her head. After a second, she finally had the wherewithal to grab Jenkins' collar, holding the dog back as he continued to bark.

'I said back that way, you freckled fancy.' It glanced at Jenkins. 'And you can shut up.' It gnashed its teeth and Jenkins hunched lower, barks escalating. The creature gave a rumbling, sighing hiss and rolled its eyes.

'*Jenkins!*' Kenzie hissed. She glanced behind the creature, to where the factory was.

'Ah, ah, ah, back, back, back,' the creature tittered, waddling forward.

'Fucking don't.' Kenzie stepped backwards, hauling Jenkins with her. The creature stopped, blinking up at her with its too-round eyes. Kenzie stared. They had plenty of people trawling Kirkall in fae garb, but this was on another level. 'What do you want?'

'Precious, precious coin.'

'What?'

'And I will have it, oh yes. Court pay well, very well. Once you get away.' Its eyes fell to Jenkins. 'Leave mutty. Tough meat. Good for the teeths.'

When the pupils of his eyes dilated, that was all Kenzie needed to spur herself into action. She made a quick arc around the creature, pushing Jenkins along too.

'Oh no, oh no, oh no!' the creature cried out gravelly. It continued to mutter behind her, 'Oh, the lady won't like this. Oh no she won't. She'll have my head, my head she'll have. Stupid, sniveling, weaselly human.' The creature growled and Kenzie broke into a sprint.

'Come on, Jenkins,' she gasped. The dog let out one last bark and darted ahead.

They made it to the grounds of the factory. She rounded the first wall and ducked into an alcove to catch her breath. She could see the factory proper in front of her.

Bringing her phone out, she hastily messaged Sierra, *Where are you??*

She was still waiting for a reply when she heard a whistle. Looking up, she spotted Sierra in the doorway to the factory in front of her, the dilapidated door heavily tagged with graffiti. She smiled and gave Kenzie a little wave.

Kenzie took a couple of relieved steps towards her before pausing. She looked at her feet. The ground—was the ground shaking? She took one more step forward when a rumbling sound swelled from beneath her. Jenkins let out a piercing howl just as Kenzie's phone fell from her hand, smashing on the concrete. She glanced up at Sierra in alarm. The girl was peering at the wall next to her, where a fissure was snaking its way up the stone.

Suddenly the chimney was falling from the sky. Kenzie watched it collapse, toppling into the quarry beside it.

'Sierra!' she cried, pointing at it. Sierra looked up, just as the building fell on her.

Kenzie didn't have time to scream with the storm of dust hurtling towards her. She ducked around a wall, shouting for Jenkins who she couldn't see anymore. Covering her mouth, she waited a few seconds with her eyes tightly closed before peering around the wall, letting out a smothered wail at the sight of the razed factory. The whole thing—collapsed. Folded in like a house of cards.

The rumbling had stopped. She rounded the wall, white dust settling over her. She spotted her phone and fell to her knees. Beneath the heavy layer of dust, the screen was smashed. She punched the power button but nothing happened

'Fuck,' she whispered, standing back up. Her legs nearly gave out from shaking so much. 'Sierra!'

A whine sounded from beside her and Jenkins limped up, his black fur coated in grey. He was shaking like a leaf.

'Jenkins,' Kenzie breathed, pulling him to her side. She looked back at the mess of white stone, glass and spiky, metal supports, eyes flitting wildly, trying to catch sight of Sierra or any of them.

'Come on,' she said shakily. 'We have to go.'

In tears now, Kenzie jogged back out towards the woods. She was so far away from any help and the thought made her sob.

They came across the creature again, sitting on a felled tree. At the sight of her running past, it jumped up.

'Oh!' it howled. 'Oh, she lives, she lives. Yippee!'

'Phone a fucking ambulance!' she screamed back. It was

then she saw the ribbon on its smallest finger, tattered and frayed, but blue like hers.

She must have been running for ten minutes before she finally came across a man in the woods.

'Help!'

The man turned. His dogs, two large akitas, barked, startled by her sudden appearance. The man frowned at her. 'You alright, love?'

Kenzie shook her head. She couldn't breathe. She pointed towards the factory. 'My friends. They were in the factory. It's just collapsed.'

'Oh Jesus, was that what that noise was?' He fumbled for his phone. 'I thought they were blowing up the quarry or something.'

'Quick,' Kenzie gasped. She pulled hair away from her face, willing her breathing to slow as the man called *999*.

'…yep, ambulance I think,' Kenzie heard the man say. 'There's kids in there, she says…'

Kenzie bit her lip until she tasted blood.

'Right, that's that done.' The man pocketed his phone. 'Let's go and see what's what then.'

By the time the emergency services arrived, the man, as well as a few others who'd heard the building collapse, had hauled enough rubble away to find a bag, a shoe, a red jacket and what could be the remains of a mangled leg. Kenzie watched it all from the alcove, holding onto Jenkins. The dog had finally stopped shaking.

After the police had gotten her statement, they loaded her in a car and drove her home. Kenzie opened the door as if in a dream. Rubble dust from her shoes sugared the floor.

Catching sight of her, Kenzie's mum let out a cry and ran over. Her cheeks were streaked with tears.

'Oh, Kenzie! I saw it on the news. They said there were kids in there and I thought for sure it was you and then I saw you on the telly. Are you alright? I've been ringing and ringing.'

Kenzie shook her head, covering her face. The tears came then, swift and hot. Arms came around her, holding her tight. 'They're all dead,' she sobbed.

'Oh, love.' Her mum rubbed her back, kissed her hair. 'Oh, my baby girl.'

CHAPTER 32

A vigil was held a few days later. They set it up on the small green in the town square. Kenzie turned up late on purpose, but she could still feel the eyes of the parents on her. They all knew she had been there.

Why hadn't she died too? those eyes asked. *Why my child?*

Kenzie curled her hands to fists. Every fibre in her being wanted to turn, to run home and hide. But she stayed. For Sierra. For all of them.

Flowers were laid, pictures and candles and small, personal mementos. Throughout it all, Kenzie shook with the will to keep back tears. She stepped up to the memorial; it spilled almost onto the pavement now. Clasped in her hand was a necklace Sierra had made for her three years ago. She wasn't even sure she had it anymore until she found it in a box at the back of her wardrobe. She didn't remember ever wearing it and felt guilty for that now. It was made up of beads—blues and purples, Kenzie's favourite colours.

Sierra had given it to her the day after they'd first had sex. Kenzie's first time with a girl, Sierra's first time ever. They were sat in the milkshake bar which had opened for all but six months in their shitty town. Sierra sat sucking hers, a weird smile on her face, jiggling her leg beneath the table. Kenzie remembered feeling annoyed, annoyed but definitely in love.

'What?' she asked, reaching a hand beneath the table to stop the jiggling.

Sierra had then chucked the necklace at her. 'Made it for you,' she said.

Kenzie found a framed photo of Sierra and hooked the necklace over the corner. She lingered, trying to think of something to say. Nothing came. Nothing seemed enough. Kenzie turned and headed for home.

ॐ ॐ

When she saw the two police officers at her door, her heart fell. What did they want to talk to her about? she wondered. Asa? The accident that killed every one of her friends? At this point it was a toss-up. Kenzie felt an incredulous giggle rise up.

'Excuse me,' she said.

The two officers parted for her.

'Mackenzie Taylor?' one of them asked, a woman. Her hat was too big for her head and fell into her eyes. She pushed it back, watching Kenzie.

Kenzie stuck her key into the door. 'That's me.'

'May we come in? We're here to talk to you about Asa Beckford. We called on the phone.'

'I remember. Yeah, come in.'

She led them to the living room. She didn't bother with tea and pleasantries. She wanted it over with as quick as possible. She had the story down pat now, having gone over it so often, in her own mind, with her mum, with Carrie.

'So this girl,' the woman was saying. She looked up at Kenzie to confirm, 'Earlie?' Kenzie nodded. 'You've not seen her since that night?'

Kenzie shook her head. 'No, I haven't. Although…' Kenzie remembered the note she'd left a couple of days ago. 'I have heard from her.'

'You have? Via social media, texting?'

'No, a note. She doesn't have a phone. We've been leaving notes for each other all summer. By a tree just up the road.'

The female officer shuffled forwards on the sofa. 'So, she must be nearby then, to be leaving notes.'

'Guess so. Don't know where she's been staying though. Can I go get it?'

The male officer nodded. 'Please.'

Kenzie jogged up the stairs. Jenkins ran up with her. In her room, she took out her diary and turned to the last page she'd written on, where she'd left the note. It wasn't there. She flicked through the pages, then upended the book, shaking out it out. Kenzie let out a frustrated sigh. It wasn't in her drawer, nor on her desk.

Back in the living room, she threw up her hands, sitting back down.

'It's gone. It's not where I left it.'

The woman pursed her lips, looking disappointed. 'Anywhere it could be?'

'No, I remembered where I put it and it's not there anymore. I just looked.'

'Well, what did this note say?'

'It said...' Kenzie put her eyes to the ceiling, thinking. 'It said something like, *I've not forgotten you and I'll see you soon.* And then something which I didn't get. *You'll never have to see those dirty flies again,* or something like that.'

'Dirty flies?'

'Yeah, I don't know what that means. She's always doing little riddles like that.'

'Could she have been talking about Asa?'

Kenzie frowned. 'I don't think so. How would that make sense?'

'Well, we don't know Mackenzie, that's why we're asking.'

Kenzie opened her mouth to reply when the front door opened. Her mum came into the living room, her face creased with concern. She'd just been to a hospital appointment in the city; it'd broken her heart that she couldn't make the memorial.

'They're here about Asa,' Kenzie said dully.

Kenzie's mum scoffed lightly. 'You know he went missing almost a week ago, don't you? Took you lot long enough.'

Dropping her handbag beside the chair Kenzie was sitting on, she came to perch on the arm, arm around Kenzie.

There was silence whilst the officers consulted their notes.

'What now?' Kenzie asked into the quiet. 'Have you checked CCTV and things like that? Do you know Asa is gay?'

'Do you think that's relevant?' the woman asked.

'I don't know. There's been a few attacks on gay men in Leeds over the years. Asa was pretty obviously gay.' Kenzie shrugged. 'Could be a hate thing.'

The male officer nodded. 'We're looking into all angles.'

As they gathered up their notes, Kenzie's mum took her gently by the chin and turned her face up to her. 'Just been to the vigil, love?' She stroked under her puffy eyes with a thumb.

Kenzie nodded.

'We heard about the incident that happened here a few days ago,' the woman officer said awkwardly, watching them. 'Did you know anyone involved?'

Kenzie gritted her teeth. 'Yeah. I did.'

'Well, I'm very sorry about that.'

'Well, don't let her be any more sorry,' her mum said. 'Find that boy.'

❧ ❧

Kenzie stared at the accommodation offer, feeling numb. They'd put her up in Kestrel Court, a gated hall of residence, a five-minute walk away from the university. Nice little courtyard. Flat 3a. Room 1.

Kenzie's bottom lip began to tremble. How far away she felt from that life now. It represented a time before, when everything was normal and boring, and a future she didn't feel part of anymore. And Earlie…

Kenzie's chest hitched. 'Fuck,' she cried, covering her face with her hands.

'Kenzie, love?' Her mum came into the room. 'Baby, what's wrong?'

'Everything's just shit,' she sobbed. 'Everything.'

Her mum held her until she cried herself out. Until she felt numb again. Sniffing, she pulled away. Her mum came to perch on the edge of her desk beside her.

'Tell you what, love,' she said gently, tucking hair behind her ears, 'why don't you go stay with your da for a few days, hm? Get away from here for a bit. Police have spoken to you about Asa now. Might be good to go sort your head out before you start at uni.'

Kenzie nodded, wiping her nose. 'Yeah. That sounds good.'

'Alright, love.' Kenzie's mum stood. 'I'll go call your father.'

CHAPTER 33

Kenzie leaned her head against the train window as it pulled out from the station, the vibrations of the pane numbing her face. As the train rolled through the countryside, her eyes found Harmon Blythe's hill, blooming now with purple heather.

Her heart constricted. The last time she saw that hill, she had her arms around Earlie, and they were just about to rescue a baby rabbit and everything was lovely and bright and exciting.

It seemed she was out of tears because the only feeling she felt at that thought was a dull, insidious anger. Where the fuck was she? Why was the mere thought of her enough to make her feel crazy? Kenzie hadn't even bothered to leave a note by the tree this time. By the time she got back, Earlie would probably be gone forever, if she wasn't already.

She knew it was barmy thinking, even considering the possibility that she had something to do with the factory collapse. It was an accident, a shitty, awful, tragic accident, but an accident nonetheless. Simply a wrong time, wrong place kind of thing.

But then she got thinking about other things—like that creature in the forest that she was coming to believe wasn't human after all, or the night Asa went missing, or even that time Earlie stole a fucking bird. Growing up in Kirkall Bridge had clearly addled her mind, all that talk of fairies and goblins and magic. Not healthy. She would never work that bloody trail again.

She felt more stable once ensconced within Manchester's city centre. There was something soothing about a big city full of strangers, where no one knew her and she knew no one. It wouldn't be like that come September but for now, she let that nice, lonely feeling wash over her whilst she waited for the bus.

It was early evening by the time she pulled up to her dad's house—a small semi-detached bungalow in a less than desirable neighbourhood. She walked through the tiny front lawn, stepping over potted plants and colourful toadstool ornaments. It was a stark contrast to his next-door neighbour's drooping fence and line of lager cans sitting atop the electricity meter box. It was kind of like that around here, you had to take the good with the bad.

Kenzie knocked on the door and waited.

It opened all of five seconds later and her dad was there, booming, 'Why you knocking for, you daft thing?'

Kenzie shrugged, heart lifting at the sight of him. He was dressed in a t-shirt Kenzie had gifted him one Father's Day, the blue one which said *Dad. The Man. The Myth. The Legend.* It was about five years old now, faded, with holes in the fabric around his stomach.

'Get in here then.'

Her dad stepped back, and Kenzie entered, dropping her bag in the hallway. She looked up at him and smiled, feeling that same awkwardness she did every time it had been too long since she'd last visited.

'Hey there, monkey,' he said, opening his arms. Kenzie fell into them, wrapping her arms around his large body and squeezing hard.

'Naw,' her dad crooned. 'Your ma told me what happened back home.' He patted her back. 'I'm sorry, kid.'

'Yeah,' Kenzie said, voice muffled against his t-shirt. 'Me too.'

He patted her one last time before stepping away. 'Go on. Chuck your stuff in your room. I'll go make us a brew.'

He disappeared into the kitchen. 'Or do you want a beer? Keep forgetting you're eighteen now.'

In her room, Kenzie grinned. 'Tea's good, Dad. Thanks.'

ॐ ॐ

'So, you wanna talk about it?'

Kenzie stirred her tea, scraping down the crystals of sugar on the inside of her mug. She didn't take sugar anymore, but her dad always insisted. She didn't mind. It reminded her of when she was a kid and her mum had just started letting them meet alone, her dad having suddenly expressed an interest in her.

He loved her dearly but hadn't had a clue about how to care for a small girl. He'd bring her to the pub and let his friends buy her packets of crisps and she'd fall asleep over their laps while he played darts. He'd let her eat all the sugar-filled foods she asked for and then wonder why she wouldn't settle to sleep at night. One time, he even took her to the building site when the manager was away. One of the lads had given her a hi-vis jacket and hard hat and they all laughed as she paraded up and down the foundation of whatever building they were constructing.

Kenzie licked her spoon then set it on the magazine-filled side table next to her.

'I've been doing a lot of that to be honest,' she said. 'They've set me up with a therapist. Because I was there when it happened and stuff.'

'Oh, they have? Good stuff. Good stuff.'

Kenzie murmured noncommittally.

'Your ma also mentioned some girl you've met.'

Kenzie smiled at his abashed tone. He was staring into his mug, red creeping up his neck. God bless his heart; he really did try with her.

'Yeah, not sure it's going anywhere though. Not seen her for a while now.' *And I also think she might have something to do with my best friend's disappearance and possibly the death of all my*

171

friends, but she decided to keep that to herself.

'She pretty?'

'Stunning.'

Her dad smiled proudly. 'Thatta girl.' He wiggled another biscuit from the packet laying on his lap and dunked it. 'So, Frankie's got a new bird.'

'Oh yeah?'

Kenzie's dad nodded. 'Aye. She's still married though with little kids, so it's all a bit of a drama. Won't last, like.' He shrugged. 'Oh! And did I tell you that crazy old bat up road finally popped her clogs?'

Kenzie shook her head, happy to let him prattle on. It was nice to listen to someone else's life, instead of rehashing hers all the time. Kind of macabre, how another person's drama could be her tonic.

આ ∞

Across the road from the chippy, a staffie pissed against a lamppost, then trotted up to a nearby bin, sniffing at the polystyrene containers littering the floor beside it. The thing had a collar on but there was no owner in sight. Looking up and down the road, Kenzie wondered if the dog was lost.

She kicked her foot up to the wall of the chippy behind her, keeping an eye on it. Her dad was inside, ordering their tea. The small takeaway was busy and Kenzie had opted to wait outside; indoor places with lots of people made her nervous these days.

'Here we are then.'

Kenzie straightened from the wall as her dad came over, carrying a plastic bag and a smaller one made of brown paper for their pots of mushy peas and gravy. Kenzie nodded over to the dog.

'Should we try and find its owner?'

Her dad glanced at it and shook his head. 'Nah, leave it. They run wild around here like the foxes. Damn irresponsible owners. Here, hold these will you.'

Kenzie took the two cans of dandelion and burdock held out to her and balanced them against her chest as they began their short walk back to the house.

With her feet up and the telly on and a plate of fish and chips in front of her, Kenzie should have felt chill and happy hanging out with her dad as she usually did. She only felt slightly removed (dissociation, her therapist had coined it) and a bit restless that she should be out doing something—anything—rather than carrying on as if everything was normal.

The day before last, she had put plastic-covered pictures of Asa up around Kirkall Bridge, just in case, and visited the memorial site to put fresh flowers down and pick up the odd drink can some bastard had thrown down. And then every evening, she went out to the tree on the fairy trail and replaced her old messages with new ones. It never seemed enough though, when it never amounted to anything and nothing changed.

'You're picking at your food. What's up?'

Kenzie pursed her lips, glossy with grease. 'Not had much of an appetite lately. Thinking of my dead friends puts me right off, you know?'

'Yeah well, eat up. You're getting too skinny, my girl.'

Kenzie glanced at her so-not skinny body and smirked. 'Oh yeah.'

Her dad added more salt and vinegar to the last of his chips. 'What's on your mind then?'

Kenzie chuckled humorously. 'You know, this is super fucked up, but out of everything, the thing I think about the most is that girl I was seeing.'

Her dad grunted. 'What's her name again?'

'Earlie.'

'Earlie.' His lips twisted. 'Not keen. Well, I wouldn't worry. Plenty of fish and all that, especially what with that Canal Street.'

Kenzie laughed. 'Gay Mecca, is it?'

Her dad shrugged. 'You know more about that stuff

than me.'

Kenzie nodded, nibbling on a chip. 'Yeah, I dunno. Relationships always go to shit, don't they?'

'Too young for that kind of thinking.' He pointed his fork at her. 'You're a strapping lass. Any girl or guy would be lucky to have you.'

'Just girls, Dad.' She put down her fork and began folding the paper back around her food. It was cold now. 'Thanks for the pep talk but I think I'm gonna take a leaf out of your book and stay single from now on.'

෩ ෨

'We could put a film on,' her dad suggested a bit later on.

Kenzie had just finished washing their cutlery. She dried her hands on a dishtowel and nodded. 'Sure.'

She took her place on the sofa whilst her dad flicked through the film choices on the telly.

'There's that new horror,' he said, 'you know the one with the witches and that goat creature thing. Or do you want something a bit lighter?'

'Always down for a horror.'

'Alright.' He selected the film and waited for it to load.

'Pause it a sec,' Kenzie said. 'If we're going to do this, I need some snacks.' She stood up. 'Shop up the road will still be open, won't it?'

Her dad nodded. 'Shuts at 11, that one.'

'Cool. Want anything?'

'Could you get us some chocolate please, love. My usual. And a bottle of pop.'

'Any crisps?'

Her dad shrugged. 'Wouldn't say no.'

Kenzie picked up her new phone and wallet. 'Back soon.'

Outside, night had fallen and a wind had picked up. Kenzie buttoned up her jacket. It suddenly felt like autumn.

Besides a young lad scouting the beer shelf, Kenzie was the only one in the shop. She picked her foods quickly and took them to the counter.

Back out on the pavement, she paused to rearrange the carrier bag, stuffing her wallet into her back pocket.

As she retightened her fingers around the plastic handles, a gust of wind threw hair into her face and when she tossed her head to dislodge it, her eyes caught a flash of white-blonde hair.

Her steps halted. She stood there, staring at Earlie and wondering if she was hallucinating. She'd been thinking all kinds of weird shit lately, but the vision held firm. She stood just on the edge of the road, clothed in a dress which fluttered in the wind, and Kenzie's old jacket.

The force in which her heartrate spiked almost panicked her. 'How are you here?' she asked, voice not betraying the turmoil within.

Smiling only slightly, Earlie raised the little finger of her right hand, where a blue ribbon was tied in a bow. Kenzie frowned, absently toying with her own. She hadn't taken it off, the only connection she had to this girl.

'Do you have any time for me?' Earlie asked, lowering her hand back to her side.

Kenzie glanced down at the bag in her hand. 'One sec,' she said. 'Let me just text my dad.' After she'd done that, she looked up and down the dark street. 'This way. Pretty sure there's a park around here.'

As they reached the small playpark, it began to rain.

'Let's go under there,' Kenzie said, nodding to a domed metal structure on the edge of the playground.

They sat down in the woodchips. Kenzie took out her phone, turned on its torch and laid it screen down. The harsh light drew shadows on Earlie's face. She looked so somber, so serious. Kenzie felt a stab of panic. She wanted that lightness back, that wonder.

'So, where have you been?' she asked. 'I've been leaving you notes.'

175

'I had to go home.'

'Do you know where Asa is? He's missing, you know. Like the police are looking for him and everything. He went back with you that night.'

'Your friend is well. He is with the court.'

Kenzie frowned. 'What? What does that mean?'

'Kenzie, there's a world apart from here. A world I am from.'

Kenzie held up her hands. 'Look, you're gonna have to speak properly right now. I don't have time for your riddles and elusions anymore. Tell me what the fuck happened to Asa.'

'He is with my sisters.'

Kenzie threw up her hands. 'Who the fuck are your sisters? Who even are you Earlie? Why does all this strange fucking shit keep coming back to you?' Kenzie gripped the hair on her head. 'I feel like I'm losing my mind.'

Earlie smiled, but it was sad. 'It is love.'

'No.' Kenzie pointed at her, shaking her head. 'It's not love. I know that now. It's some fucking infatuation, obsession. It feels horrible. It's not love. We don't even know each other. I literally know *nothing* about you.' Kenzie was trembling. 'You know what? Sometimes I wish I'd never bloody met you.'

Earlie's face shuttered. 'Do not say that, Kenzie.'

'Don't tell me what to do.' Kenzie turned away. She had to. Damn Earlie's beauty. She hated her. She wanted to crush her in her arms and kiss her until she couldn't think anymore, and she hated her.

'All my friends died, you know. Last week.' Kenzie turned back and watched Earlie carefully. It didn't make any sense. She knew Earlie couldn't have anything to do with it, and yet… 'They were in a building,' she continued, 'and it fell on them. You weren't there. I could have done with you with me.'

'They were not your friends. They hurt you.'

'Fucking hell, Earlie. I didn't want that!'

176

Earlie tilted her head. 'I thought you did. You said.'

Kenzie shook her head. 'What the hell is wrong with you? Sometimes you can be so sweet and other times you're a total psycho. My friends are dead.'

Earlie frowned. 'Now you are hurting me.'

Kenzie sighed. She regarded Earlie, feeling strangely heartbroken. 'This is all done, isn't it? Us, I mean.'

Earlie nodded slowly. 'It has to be.'

'Yeah.'

Silence stretched between them.

'Kenzie,' Earlie finally said. 'I want to be true with you.'

Kenzie hit her head back against the metal structure. 'What now?'

'You have to promise not to run.'

'What?'

'Promise.'

Kenzie straightened back up. 'Alright,' she said. 'As long as you're not about to murder me or something.'

Earlie smiled, shaking her head. 'I would never want to hurt you.'

'Then what?'

'It would be better, I think, if I showed you.'

Earlie put her eyes to the ground. In the white light of the phone torch, Kenzie saw her pupils dilate. It reminded her of that creature in the woods, the one with the blue ribbon around its finger. Kenzie looked down at hers and then over at Earlie's. A sick, panicky sensation clawed its way up inside her as that feeling of knowing increased. She opened her mouth to say something, anything, when the world lurched, her vision breaking up into waves.

When it settled, she wasn't looking at Earlie anymore, the pretty girl she'd had sex with and cuddled with and baked fairy cakes with, but a creature just as unworldly as that thing in the woods. Her skin was translucent, showing a map of blue and purple veins, her eyes lilac and lips corpse-pale.

Kenzie froze for only a second. Then she jumped to her

177

feet. Earlie seized her wrist. Kenzie tried to pull away but was held quick by the tingling wave travelling up her arm. Her heart sped up, matching the pulsing starting up below. She gasped. Earlie leaned forward and pressed her lips to hers. Kenzie stopped breathing. She'd never felt so turned on and so appalled in her whole life.

'Oh, precious Kenzie,' Earlie whispered, brushing their noses. 'Do not forget your promise.'

Kenzie sagged back, strangely languid. 'Why do I feel so still?' She put a hand to her chest. 'I feel like my heart might stop.'

A look of sympathy crossed Earlie's face. 'It will pass.'

Kenzie could only stare. As she did, as she got used to the strangeness of Earlie's face, it finally dawned on her how beautiful she was. How truly, unnaturally, strangely beautiful.

'Are you real?' she whispered.

'Yes, my love.'

'I feel...I feel...' Kenzie swallowed. 'It all feels wrong. This whole summer...' Kenzie put a hand to her head. 'Sorry, my brain isn't taking this in very well.'

A sound from outside the dome made her look up. It sounded like horses, hooves pressing into the woodchips, a tinkling of reins, a snuffling snort.

Earlie glanced out of the archway.

'What's going on?' Kenzie asked. There were eyes peering into the dome. Round eyes, slitted eyes. Kenzie couldn't see the bodies they belonged to.

Earlie turned back to her. 'It is time I go home now.'

'Oh,' was all Kenzie could say.

Earlie smiled. Kenzie thought she could see tears in the corners of those purple eyes. 'Let me hold you one final time, sweet mortal.'

Kenzie held still as Earlie's arms came around her, trying not to breathe in that alien, mulchy smell of her. Though she'd braced herself, the same tingling happened. It was like ice forking up her veins, so cold it almost burnt. Earlie

178

kissed her head. Then she put her mouth to Kenzie's ear
and breathed the words,

> *Goodbye my love, my mortal sweet,*
> *I return to the hill of soil and peat.*
> *To stop the tears and heartbreak-plea,*
> *tomorrow you will wake to no thoughts of me.*
> *For now, I take your memories true,*
> *and only if we glimpse the other,*
> *will they find their way back to you.*

CHAPTER 34

Earlie watched Kenzie pick her way across the woodchips, fingers loose around the plastic carrier bag she held. A bottle of something had fallen from it and lay inert on the ground, rain plinking on its plastic surface. Kenzie didn't seem to notice.

This would be the last time she would see her mortal. Earlie stared at her retreating figure. She willed for tears that would not come. She begged for her heart to break but it only ached, and even that ache was almost pleasant.

Only when Kenzie was lost to the night did Earlie turn and accept the hand up to the waiting horse, his hide as orangey-black as the polluted sky above.

She felt Risarial's arms come around her as she reclaimed the reins.

'She never loved me,' Earlie said.

Risarial's arms tightened. 'I told you,' she said. 'Complicated, messy creatures.'

Looking over her shoulder, Earlie said, 'It is your turn now, sister.'

Risarial smiled but it was grim. 'Yes. Yes, it is.'

ONE MONTH LATER

Kenzie jammed her dorm room door open with the grey rubber wedge she'd unearthed from under the doormat. She was alone in the flat at the moment but she knew from the accommodation messaging board that the other three girls would be arriving later—two today and the last tomorrow.

'Make sure you make friends,' her mum had warned her, as if Kenzie needed any help in that department. She could chill with pretty much anyone. Still, the open door would help to give off that impression.

She pulled her suitcase into the middle of the floor, smiling at the potted fern plant on her desk— 'Fake, because if you're anything like me, a real one would be dead within a week,' her dad had said when gifting it to her.

It was strange watching her mum and dad being parents together. A taste of another life, maybe. But they'd made it work, even going out for lunch as a family once they'd dropped Kenzie's stuff off at her room.

She knew they were both worried about her; her dad had pretty much freaked when she'd woken up at his that morning with great black holes in her memory.

The doctors said it was probably due to all the trauma, which didn't make sense when she remembered all that stuff as clear as day. They'd sent her for scans anyway. It had all come back fine in the end, and they said her memories would probably patch in over time. Kenzie was relieved; she hadn't wanted to defer her uni placement.

She put her clothes away first, stuffing them into the tiny wardrobe at the foot of the bed. She hadn't taken much with her at all, only her suitcase of clothes, box of kitchen and cleaning equipment and another box of personal stuff. She kicked the box of cleaning stuff out into the hall to deal with later.

Sitting down on the bed, she pulled the final storage box towards her and lifted the flaps. Her photos were on top— one of her parents she'd taken on one very awkward birthday a couple of years back; another of Asa which made her heart constrict to look at and lastly, one of her squeezing the life out of Jenkins. Kenzie smiled. She was going to miss that stupid dog.

Next came her rolled up posters. She pulled out the first and unfurled it. It was of two women, naked apart from the underwear they wore on the lower parts of their bodies. One was butch, tall and broad, towering over her smaller counterpart. The second girl, the one who had made Kenzie purchase the thing in the first place, was slender and blonde, her hair brushing the skin of her lower back.

Kenzie stared at her for a while, the sight of her hauntingly familiar.

She didn't think on it too long; the connections were never made. It used to make her feel crazy but the doctors had said not to try too hard. Instead, she turned her eyes to the bare white walls, wondering where best to tack it. She knew it was kind of crude but fuck it, she was single and didn't care who knew her preferences.

At the bottom of the box was her diary. She didn't know why she'd taken it; she hadn't written in the thing since January, but she figured new beginnings and all that. Sitting back on the bed, she absently flicked through it, reading through the entries. When she got to July of this year, she frowned.

I met this girl today—

It was scribbled out but still legible. What girl? Surely she'd remember if she had met someone. She continued on,

184

breath catching when she caught sight of Asa's name.

She'd written about a party she didn't remember. When the paragraphs turned into a spiel about some girl called Earlie, Kenzie's heart began thumping. She didn't remember any of this. It was like reading someone else's fiction. Had she made it all up or was this real? Where the hell was this girl now?

Her head spiked with pain. She put a hand there, reminding herself again that there was no tumour, no problems at all. When she got onto reading about this girl's looks, her white hair and tiny shoulders, Kenzie glanced up at the poster she just stuck to her wall. Jesus, was she losing it?

She zoomed through the rest of the diary, shaking her head at the craziness she was reading. When she couldn't bear it any longer, Kenzie pulled over her laptop and brought up her social medias.

She searched them all. No trace of any Earlie. So, she wasn't real. Kenzie felt weirdly down about that. But why had she written all that stuff? She read again the entry from the night Asa disappeared, when this girls' friends had turned up and whisked her away, when the boy Asa kissed suddenly had a face of a girl, when the ground reached up and pulled at her feet so she couldn't follow.

It reminded her of a story in Blythe's book, where a love-stricken boy had so wanted to follow his fairy love to the hill that she'd had to bind him to a tree with vines, stuffing his mouth with nettles so he'd stop calling after her. At the end of that story, the boy had died, suffocated on leaves.

Almost without thinking, she brought up a new tab and navigated to Kirkall's community forum. She'd never visited it before, didn't have an account, but she knew there was a thread on all things Harmon Blythe—his lore and essays and sightings recurrent in the area. She was surprised to see the latest encounter was only posted in May of this year.

She clicked on it.

'Hello.'

Kenzie looked up. A girl stood at her door. Her dark hair was pulled up into a tight ponytail and there was a shy smile on her face.

Kenzie managed a shake smile back. 'Hey, you alright?'

The girl nodded and stepped into the room. 'Just us so far?'

'Yeah, looks like.'

'Cool. Can I...?' She gestured to the bed.

'Yeah sure.' Kenzie patted the space beside her. 'I'm Kenzie, by the way.'

'Emma.' The girl sat down. 'So,' she began, eyes drifting to the poster on Kenzie's wall, 'where have you come from?'

Kenzie shoved the laptop away from her and turned towards her new flatmate. She hoped she wasn't aware of how quickly her heart raced or how sweaty she suddenly was under her arms.

Just before she'd shut the laptop lid, her eyes had caught the crosshatch drawing attached to the post. It was of a creature, with bark-skin and round eyes. The creature in the birch forest, the one with the blue ribbon on its finger. Someone else had seen it too. It was fucking real.

☙ ❧

Later that night, as she listened to the music and the quiet laughter of her flatmates drinking in the kitchen, Kenzie sat at her desk with her computer in front of her. Her fingers were flying over the keyboard, eyes flitting back and forth over the submission box she was entering into.

She almost felt feverish, typing out the story of the girl she'd supposedly met over the summer, referring back to the disjointed paragraphs in her diary.

When she was done, she sat back and read over her message, fingers still hovering over the keys.

Then she added one last line: *Can fairies take away your memories?*

TURN THE PAGE TO READ THE FIRST TWO CHAPTERS OF

❧ RISARIAL ❧

THE NEXT BOOK IN THE SISTERS OF SOIL SERIES.

CHAPTER 1

Risarial wended her away across the ridgeline, booted feet clacking loudly on the paved path. The moon was full, licking at the edges of wispy clouds and vying with the dome of light emanating from the city at the base of the ridge.

She had waited for the moon, needing its benignant light to guide her to the cluster of boulders she sought tonight. The way they loomed up against the light-polluted sky reminded her of a slumbering dragon, a relic from a world mostly forgotten. Risarial smiled wryly. She was from that world too.

She came across the first of the stones and slowly picked her way over them, frowning each time her long black gown caught under her feet—she couldn't wait to be rid of the damn thing.

Her keen eyes found the gash in the boulder she'd made using a pen knife stolen on one of her trips. Hunkering down, she regarded the base of the boulder before rolling up her sleeves and beginning to dig.

Slowly, she unearthed an array of objects—a large duffel bag, a plastic sheaf with a mobile phone and charger coiled inside, and another packed full of human money. Risarial sneered at the last item—that, she certainly wouldn't need.

Unzipping the duffel bag with dirt-blackened fingers, she pulled out a few neatly folded items of clothing and stood up to remove her dress.

For a while, she stood naked in the light of the moon,

gazing down at the city of Manchester huddled at the bottom of the vast hills she walked upon. It looked so small from here; quiet, sleepy, though she knew it was anything but.

She pulled on a pair of jeans and a black long-sleeved shirt. Running her hands over the cotton, she allowed herself to reminisce on the last time she wore these clothes.

When the memories just as quickly soured, she set her jaw and kicked her dress into a heap beneath the boulder. The action reminded her of a human funeral and as she heaped soil back on top of it, she only hoped that signified new beginnings and wasn't a portent of doom.

❧ ❦

Stepping up into Parsonage Gardens, she fixed her eyes on the building at the end of the small green. The block of flats was all rust-coloured brick and stylish blue glass and interior lights made to imitate sunlight. Risarial didn't think it held a candle to the grand Edwardian buildings nestled up to its side, but apparently the modern flats were rented out at ridiculous prices and eagerly lapped up by the humans who leased them.

Risarial stepped up to the door and keyed in a code, shaking her head when it immediately beeped her through. The idiot hadn't even thought to change the numbers.

She took the lift to the top floor, enjoying the whooshing feeling in her stomach as it zoomed upwards.

She regarded herself in the mirror, her reflection stark beneath the fluorescent lights. Glossy black hair tumbled over her breasts, framing a long, oval face which always reminded her of her mother, no matter how much she glamoured herself. Her eyes were dark, almost black, and her lips were red though she wore no colour. A snippet of a memory flooded her mind. *You always look like you've just been kissed,* came the teasing voice, a voice which made her smile as she continued her scrutiny, running her eyes down her denim-clad legs.

She always wondered what humans thought of her when they looked at her and she wondered even more how they'd react if she showed them her true form.

The lift finally opened onto a white corridor, devoid of residents at this hour but full of traces of them—doormats and scuffs on the floor from numerous feet and the odd coffee cup which would be swiped by the cleaners tomorrow. The apartment she sought was right at the end, tucked into a little alcove.

Risarial put a hand in her back pocket, fingers closing around a key, the metal warm from her body. Then she retracted it, raising a hand to knock instead. A smirk formed on her lips—she wanted to see the shock in his face at seeing her here.

The door opened. Risarial smiled deeper, an eyebrow rising as the man's silence ticked on. He was still dressed his work suit, shoes on, tie loosened and lying askew around his neck. His face was slack with horror.

'No,' he finally breathed.

'Yes, you snivelling rat.'

Risarial stepped forward and moved him out the way, hand braced on his chest. She stood in the middle of the open-planned apartment, eyes roving over the familiar cool-coloured walls and low furniture, the lights hanging over the kitchen island and the LED waterfall feature which glowed pleasantly beside the panoramic TV.

'Please,' the man said behind her. 'You can't do this to me again.'

'Shut up,' she snapped, letting her glamour fall from her. Whatever protest the man was about to utter next froze in his throat as she turned back around.

He swallowed and in a hoarse voice asked, 'How long this time?'

Risarial could see sweat beading on his forehead.

'However long I wish.' She took a step towards the bedroom. 'Come on,' she beckoned.

'Please,' he begged again. 'I'm seeing my daughter tomorrow. It's her birthday. I can't—'

Risarial grabbed the man's arm and shoved him into the bedroom. He stopped outside the walk-in wardrobe and turned back to her beseechingly.

She nodded at the door. 'In.'

Sobbing now, the man walked into the wardrobe and towards the rail at the back that housed all his executive blazers. He backed up, shouldering his way between two jackets.

Closing her eyes to his tears, Risarial raised a hand and ran it over the man's face, careful not to touch any of that dirty wet skin. When she finally looked up, he was slumped, staring into space with a stupid grin on his stupid face. Risarial grimaced at the patch of wet trickling from his trouser leg. Turning, she exited the wardrobe, closing the door firmly behind her.

She looked around the bedroom, lip curling at the state of the rumpled bedsheets and underwear strewn across the carpet. Releasing a sigh, she bent down, plucking a pair of boxers between pinched fingers. Throwing them into the laundry hamper, she turned to a rogue sock and did the same. She would move to the kitchen next, and she wouldn't stop until the place was immaculate.

CHAPTER 2

It was growing cold. Before leaving the flat again, Risarial took a coat hidden at the back of the wardrobe. It was a woman's coat. The man—Matthew or Michael or whatever his name was—had been married once and there were a few mementos still dotted around the place. It was pitiful really.

Sliding her hands into the deep pockets of the tan-coloured trench coat, she walked back through the gardens. It was past midnight now and the place lay quiet. Heading west, she crossed the bridge over the river, taking a second to gaze into it. A nixie bobbed just below the surface, humming gently. A human couple stood at the bridge's edge, staring into the water. Though they couldn't hear the nixie's song, they were still compelled to stop and peer down.

Spotting Risarial with its large bulbous eyes, it nodded its head once before descending back into the depths. The human couple roused and continued their night walk. Briefly, Risarial wondered what choices the nixie had made to wind up here, swimming in the filth of a polluted city river.

She was soon on Chapel Street, the buildings lining it wrapped in scaffolding, the walls below tagged heavily in graffiti. She turned off onto a quieter lane, slowing her steps when she found the building she wanted. Looking around, she couldn't see anyone. She only hoped she was early and not too late. For the first time since arriving earthside, Risarial felt a welling of nerves. She stepped back into the shadow of a large bin and waited.

৵ ๙

At exactly ten past one, the girl emerged from around the corner. Risarial leant her head further back, out of the light of the streetlamp and watched.

The girl fiddled around in her bag, searching for her key. She looked just as Risarial remembered, dressed in all black—like Risarial herself usually was and something they'd bonded over the first time they'd met. She wore a light leather jacket and her hair was just as short as the last time she'd seen her.

Risarial let out a slow breath through her nose, blood tingling at the sight of this human. Part of her loathed that such a creature could have this effect on her. A bigger part, though, yearned to be recognised.

Just as the girl put the key into the door, Risarial stepped out of the shadows.

'Ruth.'

The girl looked over her shoulder. Her eyes remained blank, even as they connected with hers, but Risarial's nostrils flared at the sudden spike of the girl's heartrate. It almost made her sway.

Then Ruth laughed. 'Are you actually fucking kidding me?'

'Ruth, just listen.'

'No.' Ruth turned back to the door and opened it. 'Fuck off.'

Gritting her teeth, Risarial reached out and pulled Ruth around to face her.

'Listen to me,' she implored.

Ruth sighed, folding her arms and shucking Risarial's hand from her. 'What?'

Risarial wetted her lips. 'Ruth,' she began, voice low,

'I…despise how I left things. I've returned to…make amends. With you.'

Ruth scoffed lightly. 'What, just like that? Really? And you didn't just leave things. You majorly fucked them up.'

'I know.'

'No.' Ruth shook her head. 'I don't think you actually do. You don't have any idea what you—' Ruth released a breath, her eyes going to somewhere above Risarial's head. When she looked back, her expression was shuttered again. 'I'm seeing someone else now. I'm not interested in anything you have to say. So you can take your grovelling and fucking do one.'

A dark, black feeling slithered up Risarial's body. 'What?'

'You heard. I'm with someone else now.' She turned back towards the door. 'She's coming over in a minute and she'll kick your face in if she sees you here.'

She walked through the door, reaching a palm back to slam it shut. Much as she'd done that man, Risarial shouldered her way in after her, backing Ruth up against the wall.

She looked into Ruth's eyes. They were green now in the dingy light of the entryway. Outside, just then, they'd been grey.

'Get off me,' Ruth whispered.

Risarial debated for only a second before leaning her forehead against Ruth's and closing her eyes. 'Forgive me,' she breathed before running a hand over the girl's face, murmuring a spell. This time, she let her fingers stroke the soft, warm skin.

Ruth slumped in her arms. Risarial caught her and looked down the entryway.

'Come on,' she murmured, holding the girl tightly as they shuffled their way down the corridor. The girl moaned quietly and Risarial soothed her with a hand to the forehead. Ruth's key had fallen on the threadbare carpet. Risarial picked it up and unlocked the flat door.

She led Ruth to the sofa. She removed her boots,

197

rightened her jacket where it had rucked up beneath her and prized off all the silver stacking rings from her fingers. Beneath the jacket, Ruth wore her black work shirt. She had been working at the pub, just as Risarial had predicted.

Getting to her knees, Risarial stroked a hand over the girl's forehead, pushing back her hair.

'I vow,' she whispered, voice trembling, 'this time will be different. The next time we meet, I'll just be a stranger to you and we'll start again. We'll start right from the beginning again, okay?'

Risarial battled down a wave of grief that this girl wouldn't remember her anymore—not the tenor of her voice, their shared, secret smiles; she wouldn't remember how their bodies moulded nor all the ways they'd talked without speaking. Ruth wouldn't even know her name.

Risarial hadn't meant for it to go like this, but she hadn't seen another way. She took a breath before finishing, 'You will cease all relations with this other person, and you will never speak to them again.'

After hovering for another moment, drinking in the gentle, sleep-softened slopes of the girl's face, Risarial pressed a kiss to her head.

'Until the night we meet again.'

✦

visit **hollythornebooks.com** to join the newsletter
and keep up to date with future book news!

✦

Printed in Great Britain
by Amazon